friday morning with sun saluki

simon lowe

Grosvenor House
Publishing Limited

This book is published by
Grosvenor House Publishing Ltd
28-30 High Street, Guildford, Surrey, GU1 3HY.
www.grosvenorhousepublishing.co.uk

A CIP record for this book
is available from the British Library

ISBN 978-1-906645-12-0

This book was written for Theresa

thanks to all my friends and family
special thanks to George Cassidy

PART ONE

friday morning with sun saluki

There is a bridge in New Luddle that stretches out over a busy commuter track. Cars and trucks grumble and shit along its uneven surface but the drivers - the Dupontians - don't ever look up.

They don't ever see the boy who stands on this bridge every morning looking down.

The boy is called Sun Saluki and he likes to look for slogans. Today he sees three. They are not new to him. Sun Saluki can't remember the last time he saw a new slogan. Today he sees three:

Dupont 4 ever (thin blue ink staggered along bicep)

Dupont is all I want (white t-shirt, thick red bubble letters)

I'm a Du – who the fuck are you? (knitted red scarf stretched across rear window)

He steps down from the bridge a little disappointed. The Dupontians don't seem as interested in slogans these days. He expected a little more on his fifteenth birthday: one-five the only age to be alive.

There are no slogans in New Luddle. Away from the bridge they are uninvented, unheard, unknown. I guess you'd need a reason to have a slogan, a reason to shout out. The New Ludlows never shout, they never have a reason.

Leaving treads in the dust Sun Saluki walks away from the bridge towards home. He sees Ferry Doberman jogging. Every morning he catches a glimpse of Ferry Doberman completing his three laps of the colony. Always bursting into a sprint for the final lap, always collapsing just short of the finish. Ferry wears pale blue shorts with black cotton stripes down each side. Sweat pours

3

down his face and drips from his fingertips. He is a lissom waxwork melting in the sun. His long hooked nose drips like a faulty tap. He is utterly soaked and completely sapped. Gradually he recovers. Gradually he straightens up. Tomorrow he'll be fine.

Ferry is the talk of the colony right now. Apparently... Ferry's brother Donny told Bill Spitz that Ferry was thinking about entering a marathon. It would seem that at first Bill Spitz wasn't too impressed with this slight piece of gossip, but then Donny explained how the marathon wasn't here in New Luddle, but across the border in Dupont.

Sun Saluki can't remember the last time a resident left the colony; perhaps when he was a child, he didn't know. He wouldn't be surprised if nobody had ever left New Luddle. Why would you? He certainly couldn't think of any reasons.

Across the street Tala Pekepoo is making her way to Beth Pointer's café. Sun Saluki waves and speaks.

'Enjoy your breakfast, Tala.'

Tala waves back but does not speak. Perhaps she didn't hear. Usually she'd say hello.

Sun carries on home, kicking dust. He leaves diamond shaped treads in the ground. He too begîins to sweat in the morning heat.

Today the sun is hot. He remembers one time, up on the bridge, a Dupontian car had a sticker in its rear window that said 'hot hot hot' in big red letters. The first 'h' and last 't' were shaded by large green parasols and all the o's were pictured as blazing suns. As Sun feels the heat spread over his body, mummifying him in warmth, he thinks this would probably be a good slogan to stick onto his fifteenth birthday - hot hot hot. With green parasols and blazing suns.

He looks at his watch. It is twenty-five minutes past eight. He needs to be home soon for breakfast if he is to make it in time to meet his friends. He promised Daisy Spaniel and Fleece Dingo he'd see them by the statue of Victor Poodle no later than nine.

4

He hurries home.

In the house, Jennifer Saluki opens a kitchen window. She has laid the table with a different cloth and brought in some flowers from the garden. She turns and hugs her son.

'Happy birthday Sun, you're just in time for some tomatoes and tea.'

Tomatoes and tea is a traditional New Luddle breakfast. New Luddle grows the finest tomatoes, sun drenched, moist and sweet. It's pretty much all they live on – tomatoes and tea.

As they sit down to eat Sun Saluki notices the new cloth and the smell of fresh flowers. And he notices his mother's smile.

'This is great mum, thanks.'

'Don't be silly it's nothing. I enjoy it. Soon you'll be a man and I won't be able to...'

'I've only just turned fifteen mum...'

'Yes but before you know it you'll be in the fields, you'll be learning...'

'Sssh - please mum, I don't want to think about that, I mean... I don't know... learning... (pause) ...it's a bit early for that talk...'

'Nonsense dear, you'll be providing for this community like all the others...'

The conversation drifts. Sun Saluki doesn't want to talk anymore. Not about the fields anyway. He loves New Luddle, he knows it is the perfect society and it's right he should contribute by working the fields just like all the others but for some reason he just doesn't quite feel ready yet. He isn't looking forward to it.

Jennifer Saluki lifts the empty plates from the table. She rinses them under cold water before placing them in the sink.

'I've gotta go meet Dasiy and Fleece.'

'Ok Sun, enjoy your day.'

'Will do.'

'And Sun... love you.'

'Yeah, you too.'

He sips the last of his tea, kisses Jennifer on the cheek and picks up his schoolbag.

He rushes to the door and runs out into a wall of sun. Picking himself up he coughs from the dust and heads towards Victor Poodle.

victor poodle and the story of new luddle

Until the late eighteenth century, Luddle was just a tiny country floating between ice caps in a freezing climate somewhere north of everywhere else. Its people were few and despite their inherent good will found the conditions tough. Many were depressed and lacked motivation. Luddle was not a prosperous or happy place.

In the latter half of the 1850s a young Ludlow named Victor Poodle began to notice incremental changes in the Luddle landscape. It appeared to Victor that the icy river mouths were widening whilst the mountains shrank. The colour and brightness of Luddle was beginning to change from dull white to glistening transparency.

Water flowed at greater speeds through the villages. Previously frozen rivulets cracked open reviving water supplies everywhere. Victor Poodle could feel the tides were coming and that Luddle was in danger of being washed away.

It proved surprisingly easy for Victor to convince the population of Luddle that their country would soon be drowned and their bodies eaten by fish. This was a disheartened nation.

But in Victor Poodle they had a leader and a prophet. It wasn't long before Luddle united in support for Victor. Being the man that he was, Victor used this power not for personal gain but to open channels of debate in an attempt to find consensus among the Ludlows. After months of forums, discussions and votes it finally became clear to Victor that people generally were after the same things in life. They wanted to work the land so they could provide for themselves and each other. They wanted to live as a community rather than individuals, with an equality of resources and power that filtered through to everyone. And finally, if at all possible, they wanted to live this life in the baking hot sunshine.

When Victor told his people that their wishes would one day form reality, a few cynics laughed – but only a few. The rest of Luddle cheered for they carried enough blind faith and will for change to make anything happen.

Victor did not disappoint. He had soon drawn up plans to build a ship big enough to carry every citizen of Luddle away from the ice and into the sun.

In 1871 Dupont wasn't the leviathan of economic power it is today. Neither was it the largest country in the world, as it is today. It didn't even have the biggest army or most advanced nuclear weaponry. So when a ship captained by Victor Poodle carrying the entire population of Luddle crashed onto its North Easterly coast there were no immediate ramifications.

Fortunately, the president of Dupont at the time, Iliad S Trang, was in the process of enacting upon long awaited promises to improve democracy and internal transparency at home coupled with a new principle of détente abroad. Victor and his ship of Ludlows couldn't have picked a better Dupontian administration under which to invade.

When called to President Trang, Victor explained the situation truthfully. He gave rich and detailed accounts of his nation's woe and eventual forced upheaval. He explained the common dream in every Ludlow's heart for a peaceful self-sufficient life with only each other to depend upon and no need for wealth or power. The president admired their plan to build utopia; he admired it with great relief and granted them their wish. A small but adequate site was proposed a few miles inland from where they landed. Victor was only willing to accept under certain conditions. President Trang hesitated slightly but soon concurred after Victor reminded the president of his new commitment towards détente when dealing with developing countries. The president felt Victor Poodle would have made a canny politician and be an asset in any world government.

So the foundations were laid. The Dupontian constitution was changed disallowing any invasion or occupation of the newly formed Luddle. A trade embargo agreement was also signed making the movement of goods between the two nations illegal. Victor Poodle ensured the second Luddle would be an entirely self-governing colony with no relation to the surrounding world.

And on dusty land in hot sunshine smiling faces planted fecund farmland with every kind of fruit, vegetable and tree they could manage. Houses and a church were built, followed by a school, all for the New Ludlows as they were called. Despite there being no crime Victor insisted a small and uniquely operated constabulary be set up in case of future instances. Then in 1885 Victor Poodle died.

One year later, in the centre of what was now New Luddle, a giant statue of Victor Poodle was built, made out of the hardiest materials to ensure his presence would remain forever.

Since this time, wars have been fought, countries destroyed, races of people erased. New Luddle has remained the same. This is thanks to Victor Poodle. The prophet of doom, the prophet of hope.

Daisy and Fleece wait by Victor. They see Sun run towards them. Clouds of dust are hugging his feet. They breathe in the sweet-smelling air and then cough a little as the dust rises up to their faces.

Daisy has long black hair that falls in front of her face. She only lifts the hair from her face to smile.

When Sun arrives she has it held back in mock pony tail, so pleased is she to see her friend.

'Hey you two, sorry I'm late.'

Fleece pats Sun on the back.

'No worries, happy birthday!'

All three embrace. Fleece says they should go. Daisy is still smiling.

'Where to?'

'Beth's café.'

'Beth's?'

'Yeah, Beth's.'

Daisy interlocks her arm with Sun Saluki's.

'Come on, lets go.'

He feels her happiness. He would like to hold her hand. If Fleece wasn't here he thinks perhaps he would. He thinks this knowing that he definitely wouldn't. But anyway, it doesn't matter, interlocking arms is pretty good as it is.

'But school starts in half an hour...'

Daisy laughs. She is incredulous.

'School... school? Fuck school.'

Fleece joins in.

'Yeah come on Sun, we'll still make it in time for school.'

Sun looks to his watch for some other opinion. Nothing going. The hands slowly tell him, he's on his own with this one.

'Ok ok, fuck school, let's go.'

They walk happily, treading light steps, wiping dust from their face, smiling in the hot sunshine.

Beth's café is a very typical looking New Luddle building. Simple and efficient it has a wooden two-tier structure of horizontal panels painted white. Nobody is sure who designed the buildings in New Luddle. There is much apocryphal talk. Some say Victor Poodle designed and built every one of them himself one night whilst everyone was sleeping. It's mainly the older Ludlows who say that. The ones who'd believe any story if it had Victor Poodle in it. Younger Ludlows say a passing traveller with architectural tendencies wandered across the border without anyone noticing he wasn't a Ludlow, and designed New Luddle's buildings based on similar structures he'd witnessed in Dupont. It is said the citizens were so pleased with the results they let him stay and become a member of the colony. Nobody but the young like to believe this; nobody but the young care what is true.

Not even the young care much round here, thinks Sun Saluki. But maybe that's a good thing. Maybe that means something good, like the colony is working, or something. Sun Saluki thinks a little more about this place he has been so lucky to have grown up in.

I like the buildings in New Luddle. The long white slats that get chipped and then painted. You can always make them new again. Even the oldest buildings can be made new. Most of them have verandas so we can sit out at night. Most of us like to put flowers and plants out on the veranda. The fragrance of wood and flower and sunshine is so heady and beautiful. Beth always puts a few tables and chairs outside when it's hot like this so you can sit out and enjoy the sunshine with your cup of tea. The smell, that sweetness in the air really creates a warmth all of its own around this time of year. Daisy can get real angry about New Luddle. She calls it backward and narrow. I like it. I like the smells. I like sitting outside Beth's café. I like how in the main everyone is happy. I am Ludlow through and through. We are a happy colony, a contented people. Daisy laughs when I say this, Fleece too sometimes. She says I'm full of shit. She says: 'You wouldn't go and stand on that bridge every morning watching Dupontians if you were Ludlow through and through.' I guess she has a point - but then, not really. She's right, I like to stand on the bridge but it's just intrigue, you know? A little innocent curiosity. It's not like I ever wanna be inside the cars, I don't want to be down there at all. In fact none of this has anything to do with the real reason I go onto the bridge. I don't like talking about that.

And Daisy knows this.

When they reach Beth's café Sun Saluki is surprised to see nobody sat on the chairs outside. Sun Saluki realizes it must be late and that people have gone to work.

Daisy opens the door. Sun and Fleece follow. Inside it is empty except for the smell of strong tea and baked tomatoes. Tala Pekepoo has left. Everybody seems to have gone.

'Weird, where's Beth?'

'Dunno, let's take a seat.'

They choose the table by the window laid out for four people.

Beth is their friend. She is funny and she is nice. She lets them stay when the sign says 'closed'. She sits with them and chats when she should be working. She enjoys the chat, the meaningless jibes. She likes to reminisce. Most of the time they have no idea what she is talking about. She did tell them once why she likes hanging out with them so much. She said:

'You remind me of me, or rather you remind me of how I used to be.'

And that is the only time they have seen her cry. Except for this other time when she overheard them talking about Ned Corgi. But that was different. They didn't actually see her cry. They just knew.

Daisy and Fleece are keeping quiet.

Soon Beth is singing in the back. It takes Sun a while to figure out the tune. Beth has an awful singing voice. The melancholic gurgle of a baby crying underwater. It is all bubbles and echo.

Ha-peeeeee birthday for you, ha-peeeeeeee birthday for you,
For you-ooo Sun Saluki, ha-peeeeee birthday for you.

Daisy and Fleece stand to clap. Beth Pointer carries a large tomato cake from the kitchen and places it on the table. She reaches over and hugs Sun tightly around the shoulders. She kisses his cheek and smiles to his face.

'Happy birthday, Sun.'

'Thanks Beth, you really, really shouldn't have.'

Daisy and Fleece giggle from the inside. Beth appears flattered. They each take hold of a knife and slice the cake together. The doughy mixture crumbles easily under each blade.

'Make a wish!' screams Daisy. She is excited.

'Hey come on, how can I? What's there to wish for when you're a Ludlow?' Sun tries to keep his face straight but can't stop happiness pulling it open, 'As I believe Victor Poodle famously once said.'

Daisy and Fleece crease with laughter.

'You're so full of shit.'

'I know, but it's a good slogan, no?

'No.'

More laughter.

'Come on – let's eat cake.'

Beth dishes out a slice of tomato cake to each of them and congratulates Sun once more. She tells him off for joking at the expense of Victor Poodle. He apologizes but then perhaps wishes that he hadn't.

Beth's ok but you wouldn't normally talk about Victor Poodle like that in front of the adults. Technically speaking Victor Poodle is a messiah in this place. To the older Ludlows that is. Not so much to the kids. To the kids he's pretty much just a statue, a place for them to meet up and hang out.

Sun looks across to Daisy. She quickly wipes a tear from her eye and brushes her hair back over her face. She is very happy. Sun can tell. Fleece knows it too. He is contented with a mouthful of cake.

'Great tomato cake, Beth.'

'Thank you Fleece. You get a feel for it, you know, when you bake twenty-five a day for most of your life.'

'True, I guess you develop quite a knack.'

Beth smiles at Fleece but subtly moves her chair so that she is facing Sun.

'Anyway I don't want to talk cake anymore, I want to talk Sun. I mean fifteen. That's pretty old - you're catching me for sure.'

Sun sits back and shrugs his shoulders.

'Nah it's no big deal Beth, I'm just a day older than yesterday, just like I am every day.'

A few quizzical looks are exchanged around the table. Daisy lets out a snigger at this unexpected deluge in sagacity.

'Bullshit, what is that? Philosophy?'

Everyone laughs.

'You're a philosopher now?'

Sun reddens with embarrassment and lowers his head.

'No, course not but...'

1 4

Beth takes over. Fleece eats crumbs from his plate.

'Good. Because I'm not sure New Luddle's ready for a philosopher just yet.'

'No, but I was just saying...'

Daisy bangs down her fork to serve notice of a speech. There is tacit rolling of the eyes and 'here we go' whispers.

'New Luddle isn't ready for shit. I'll tell you what I think...'

Fleece nods his head and looks to his watch.

'Absolutely, but I'm afraid this symposium needs to adjourn for school.'

Beth stands and ushers the others up too.

'Right. Come on you lot. I'm not getting the blame this time for you being late, it's real good to see you all and I hope you enjoy your birthday Sun but now it's time to go learn something.'

'But we're going to school Beth.'

'Oh yeah, well it's time to go to school then.'

They laugh and say goodbye.

Daisy waits for the others to leave, then looks back to Beth.

They stare at each other for a few seconds in silence.

Then Daisy looks clearly into Beth's eyes and says 'I know, I know.'

Then she too leaves the café.

Beth clears the table and contemplates not Daisy or any of the kids but the five tomato cakes she has to bake before lunch.

sun saluki, daisy spaniel and fleece dingo go to school passing mrs beagle on the way

There is only one athlete in New Luddle, and that is Ferry Doberman. If Ferry Doberman stood outside Beth's café knowing he had only five minutes before he needed to be at the school, an institution located on the other side of the colony, he would try his hardest to make it, he would run like the wind, but almost certainly he would blow himself out just short of the gates. It can't be done.

'What do you reckon?'

'Easy, we don't even need to run, a fast walk and we're there ... plenty of time.'

'Daisy?'

'No chance.'

'OK. Sun? I guess you're with Daisy.'

'Why do you say that?'

'Well, are you?'

'Yeah of course it's miles away, but what's with the assumption?'

'I'm just saying...'

'Look boys, can we hurry the fuck up. You remember what today is?'

'No.'

'Yes. It's my birthday.' (big grin when spoken)

'No... well, yes... (exasperated)... as well as that it's Summer assembly with Mayor Cudrip Harrier.'

'Shit. Is it? We really can't be late for that.'

'No.'
'Shit.'
'Yes.'
'We really don't wanna be late for that.'

They run. Dust flies. They are going to be late for the summer assembly with Mayor Cudrip Harrier.

Mrs Beagle is cleaning the church doors. The dust from three rampaging teenagers makes her cough but she doesn't lose sight of the job at hand. Mrs Beagle has always ensured the St Bernard Church of Pentecostal Pantheists is spotless for when Father Lurcher gives mass on Saturday. The St Bernard church is tall and angular and decorated with flowers and fruit. Prior to Victor Poodle and the relocation to New Luddle, Ludlows didn't have any religion. Religion is difficult to conjure when you live in an icy climate. They felt alone and isolated and incapable of religion. It could be supposed that religion is about ubiquity of spirit and exposure of good will. The old Ludlows had no time for that. They just tended to shiver and moan.

But since the move all that changed. The amazing colours of fruit and vegetables and the sun and the flowers and the smells of herbs and pollen and warm air and the sight of rabbits and birds and happy people tempted the New Ludlows into believing a God must exist within nature. They found the new homeland so painfully beautiful - surely it was inhabited by God, surely this was Eden and surely God is nature and surely this is how he manifests himself to us and surely he is inside every beautiful thing that grows around us and surely this is how it must be. Surely.

Daisy Spaniel has always been amazed that New Ludlows are Pantheists. It is quite strange. Most religion is parochial. It develops out of particular groups for particular reasons. Fine. This is true also of New Luddle, they opened their eyes, saw the beautiful landscape and found God in nature. Absolutely fine. Sheer logic. Couldn't hold that against them. They didn't know any better.

'But of course they did. They had opened their eyes before,' says Daisy. 'They opened there eyes every morning to the most freezing atheistic weather imaginable. They nearly died because of the suffering iciness of their surrounding nature. I mean what did they think? That Old Luddle was some kind of celestial blip? Some place God simply forgot to inhabit? What, his bendy spirit couldn't stretch that far? It's like they decided to forget, just erased their memories for the sake of it, because it made life easier that way. A new religion is born because the past never existed and now all the shiny pieces fit into the nice little communal jigsaw that New Luddle is. Am I the only one who finds this just a little fucked up?'

Probably not. The New Ludlows case for pantheism was conceived *a posteriori*. They already experienced first hand the counter argument. They actually had some clear falsifying evidence, yet they were so blown away by the new, by the bright, by the colourful. 'They were so full of shit more like,' says Daisy. In truth, she isn't the only one. Very few young people in New Luddle are Pantheists. It's not a problem. They still go along with it all, they don't see anything wrong in it. The young Ludlows just don't believe it to be the actual truth and that's ok because neither do they care. They certainly don't mind going to church on Saturdays. The gleaming St Bernards church on Saturdays is always full at ten o'clock as everyone waits in huge expectation for Father Lurcher and his infamous sermons.

Father Lurcher. The man who brought pentecostalism to New Luddle. The man with the gift.

Mrs Beagle stands back to examine the door once more. She thinks that surely now it is clean enough. He'd never ask her to do it again now.

Sun Saluki, Fleece Dingo and Daisy Spaniel reach the mezzanine doors at the front of the school right next to the assembly room.

They are late for the summer assembly with Mayor Cudrip Harrier.

'We're late, aren't we?'

Daisy and Fleece look to their watches and give squeamish nods.

'Shit.'

'What now?'

'I don't remember anyone being late for a Mayor Cudrip Harrier assembly ... ever.'

'Me neither.'

'What'll they do to us...?'

'This is New Luddle remember, they won't do fuck all, maybe 'question our commitment.' (whiny sarcastic voice).

Daisy isn't too panicked by the situation, unlike Fleece and Sun who are shaking their legs and holding their crotches - absolutely ready to piss themselves.

'Oh no, this time we're dead... it's the Mayor the fucking Mayor, they don't let you off this sort of stuff.'

'Sun's right, it's disrespect. They hate disrespect.'

'Yeah, because do you remember that time...'

Daisy wanders to the side of the hall.

'That was bad...'

She moves towards the assembly hall doors and looks through the cracks.

'...but quite funny because I didn't even know you were...'

Daisy runs to the side of the hall once more and laughs. She runs over to Fleece and Sun.

'I don't know what made me think of it...'

'Sssshhhh.'

'Actually I didn't know he was there, so...'

'Shut the fuck up.'

'What?'

'They're coming.'

'Who?'

'Harrier and Mistress Feist.'

Just confused looks on Fleece and Sun's faces.

'They're later than we are.'

Still a sort of blankness. Then Sun.

'Fuck, let's get inside.'

They scramble through the swing doors and into the assembly hall. The room is silent. Each and every pupil is present. Thirty children stood in rows. Still and perspiring. There is a slight gasp when Sun, Dasiy and Fleece bundle in, the final morsels of oxygen inhaled. Daisy has begun to laugh more hysterically. They look to stand at the back. Shuffling through the other serious-looking pupils, they mange to find places just in time. Mistress Feist and Mayor Cudrip Harrier have entered the room and already the applause has begun.

mayor cudrip harrier gives his summer assembly

Mistress Feist is small and old. She climbs up the few wooden stairs, moves to the centre of the stage and stands behind the lectern, which is fairly tall, so only her head can be seen above it. Mayor Harrier waits in the wings. Mistress Feist has long dark hair but she always keeps it tied up in a bun with copper slides. It looks excruciating but this is her style - a vision of austerity. A few years ago there was an emergency near the school. At two in the morning a small fire broke out in a recreation zone. The whole colony dashed from their beds to see what was happening. Through the blaze Mistress Feist walked out wearing a silk night gown, her hair long and flowing. No one had any idea who this apparent phoenix of beauty was.

She gestures for the applause to stop. She takes two deep breaths, struggling like everyone else to find any air in a room that has begun to heat up even more.

'Good morning everyone, so sorry I'm late, myself and the Mayor were sat chatting in the office and we... I mean... I... completely lost track of time but thank you for your patience and superior punctuality.'

Sun, Daisy and Fleece exchange glances and clench their stomachs, desperately trying to stifle the laughter from their guts.

'Now as you know, this is a very special assembly, it is our annual summer assembly to be given by our very own Mayor Cudrip Harrier. We are extremely fortunate as the Mayor is a very busy man yet he has agreed to free up his incredibly busy schedule to spend some time this morning, speaking to you all about just what it means to be a young Ludlow and... well... erm... (forgetting) what... erm...

what the future holds for... persons like...

yourselves.... (uncertain)... who find themselves... in this... er... erm...privileged... (struggling)...

erm... position... that is... (a few coughs)... a erm... position whereby each of yourselves...'

There is a groan from the side of the stage. Mistress Feist looks across to the Mayor and nods her head. She is ruffled and slightly embarassed. Despite years of experience she has never really mastered the art of public speaking but she still enjoys the limelight and the glamour.

'Anyway without labouring on this point for too long, I'm sure the Mayor will want to... erm... explain himself... erm (pause) well... here is the Mayor. Mayor Cudrip Harrier everyone.' (the end)

Loud cheers and applause ring through the hall reverberating against the wood which swallows the sound, spitting back a strange humming drone. The Mayor raises his arms not to quieten the hall but to encourage more; he wants them to go louder. The noise soon becomes an incantation, a hypnotic chant and for a few moments it feels more like a black mass than a summer assembly. But eventually it does quieten down and before long there is silence.

The Mayor is not a tall man but he does at least stand in proportion to the lectern. His large chest is clearly visible. Today his tie is green and his shirt chequered in various colours. He has a thin but thickly bristled moustache that stretches all the way along his lip and carries on drooping down at the sides of his mouth. He is balding but what hair he does have is thick and curly. Not that you'd know looking at him now, because right now he wears the bowler hat.

Victor Poodle always wore a bowler hat. It was of course, to a certain extent, the fashion of the day but for Victor it was also symbolic. In old Luddle the weather was so cold everyone would wear a bowler hat to keep their heads warm. This even applied to small children and infants. It was protection, it was necessity. But in New Luddle the bowler hat became extraneous, totally unnecessary in this alternate climate, except for fancy dress or the threat of a chill. But Victor Poodle liked to wear his all the same. He said it symbolised how far they'd come and served as a good reminder to everyone just how bad the situation was in old Luddle when everyone had to wear a bowler hat for their own safety. He said Old Luddle was about survival and New Luddle was about choice and 'that's why I choose to wear a bowler hat; it reminds me I have the choice.'

Since his death all future mayors have been given Victor's bowler hat on their inauguration. It was usually considered to be a ceremonial quirk, none of them actually thought it appropriate to wear the hat, they usually kept it in a cupboard or a drawer to protect it from wear and tear. That was until the inauguration of Cudrip Harrier. He rarely keeps the hat in a cupboard or drawer. Like Victor Poodle, Cudrip Harrier wears the hat as a symbol. But Mayor Cudrip Harrier has a slightly different symbolism in mind to that of Victor Poodle. He regards it as a symbol of authority. A reminder that he is the Mayor, the man in charge. It shows he is someone you should listen to and take note of what they say. A truth bearer. He believes it creates awe. Originally, when he first took office it was only on the odd occasion that he'd wear it, donning it strictly in an official capacity: ceremonial appendage, display purposes, tradition and all that. But in recent years he has taken to wearing it more and more, so that now it's got to the stage where he won't leave the house without it.

Sun, Dasiy and Fleece all stand obediently and look up at the Mayor but there is nothing obedient in Daisy's face. Her teeth are clenched and her lips quiver. Breath pours out of her mouth like an army. She bows her head a little and her eyes point to the floor.

She doesn't want to look up at Mayor Cudrip Harrier but she can't help but stare straight into his eyes. She is thinking. Thinking hard about things that are not nice.

It will be twenty-three years next week since Mayor Cudrip Harrier's inauguration. As with all mayoral inaugurations in New Luddle, it passed without hiccup or splutter. It is a unique and informal constitution whereby the departing Mayor decides who his successor shall be (disclosing the name in their will) and the candidate must on the day of the funeral successfully gain a vote of confidence from the colony achieving a minimum of fifty-one percent of the Yes vote.

No Mayor has ever failed to win the vote of confidence with anything other than one hundred percent of the vote. Why wouldn't they? Jennifer Saluki always tells Sun how it was one of her proudest days. When she pressed down that rubber stamp with the full weight of her force and saw the large YES in red ink printed amongst all those other YES's on the page. That one YES was hers. Her print of affirmation. She said she felt like a citizen. Part of something. Sun asked her if she had any doubts. None she said. None what so ever.

Mayor Cudrip Harrier clears his throat. It is often clogged. Mistess Feist brings a jug of water and a glass. He swallows some water and coughs again. Swallows some water and wriggles his neck. Elevating from out of his collar. He steps forward and speaks.

'Our founder, our saviour, Victor Poodle once said – life on this colony is about choices. And he was right. Life is about choices. But how do we know which is the right choice to make? At this nascent stage in your colony life how can you be expected to make 'life choices'?

The Mayor laughs stupidly.

'The answer is simple. Make only one choice. Choose RESPONSIBILITY. Make that choice every time and you will not stray from the right path in life. We are all responsible for the success of this colony, this beautiful, efficient paradise and why? Because choosing responsibility, going down the road of responsibility has led us to where we are today. New Luddle is found at the end of this road. The most successful and prosperous society on this planet has been built based on one simple choice. This one choice that each and every citizen of New Ludlow has always made. RESPONSIBILITY.'

A slightly uncertain applause that only gains in euphoria with a few prompts from the Mayor.

...(pause)...

'Let me tell you this. You are the lucky ones. As individuals, some of whom are approaching the school-leaving age of fifteen, you are fully supported by this colony. Your life is easy. Your life is one of guarantees. It was made easy by Victor Poodle all those years ago. You will finish school, you will work in the fields and help provide in the pursuit of continued sustainability for this colony, you will reap the benefits of both your own and everyone else's labour, and you will retire with only happiness to reflect upon and happiness to look forward to. You will be healthy and you will be happy. This is the New Luddle way and all this is achieved through making one tiny little choice. But a vital choice. The one we must make everyday. The one we are proud to make everyday. RESPONSIBILITY.'

This time pupils whoop and holler, cheer and clap. They know how it works. They're not stupid (?). The Mayor stands proud.

Sun Saluki looks across to Daisy. She is standing still. He cannot see her face because of her hair. He cannot see the tears or the anger.

'Now let me talk a little, if I may, about Dupont. Apparently it is now the world's biggest superpower. But did you know that in Dupont they are surrounded by poverty, crime, *suicide* (gasps) immigration, war, greed, adultery, atheism, abortion... all sorts of things that seem to us UNIMAGINABLE. Some of you won't even recognise some of the words I just said. But it is true. They are corrupt, licentious and dissolute. These evils have no place in New Luddle. It is right these words have no meaning in New Luddle. They are not citizens like us. They are slaves. Slaves to vice and slaves to ego. They are solipsistic and depraved. Their populace is millions yet their community is one. The self. They are neighbours, yet in their morals and their ethics they could not be further away. Be thankful. You are the lucky ones. Be thankful and make the right choice.'

Before anyone has the opportunity to applaud a shout sounds out from the back of the room. It is Daisy.

'What choice?'

She moves into an aisle so that Mayor Cudrip Harrier can see it is her.

'Daisy Spaniel isn't it?' (nonchalant)

'That's right.'

'You seem upset Daisy.' (patronizing)

'I just asked a question, that's all.'

'Yes, quite right you did, you asked, "What choice?", and as I've explained the correct choice is for you and your friends to work the fields, provide for the community...'

'Yeah I know, but what's the alternative?'

'Well I don't see there is an alternative.' (irritated)

'So why do you keep saying we've got a fucking choice then?'

Lots of little gasps scamper across the room.

'Use the language of the devil again and I'll make sure there is no alternative.'

'I thought you did that already.'

'Listen... (seething anger) what are you going do, eh? Doss around and you'll be forgotten by this society, if you don't share its values, its ethic, then it will forget all about you, you'll be nothing in its eyes. This colony must work together if it is to work at all and maybe you're right, maybe that means sacrificing choice; but that is the morally correct sacrifice to make if it assures this colony continues to function as it has for over a century now. I am sure that if Victor Poodle were stood here today he would be saying the exact same thing as I am, don't you, huh? (out of breath)'

'Fuck Victor Poodle.'

Dasiy turns and walks steadily out of the assembly room which has been bludgeoned by the exchange. It stands in a comatose silence. Mistress Feist somehow finds a kind of oxygenation and steps forward.

'OK everyone back to class, the Mayor will deal with this in his own way.'

The whole school exits the assembly room including Mistress Feist, leaving Mayor Harrier stood in the same position on the stage, one hand gripped to the lectern, the other feeling his moustache. He takes off the bowler hat and begins to stare intently at the vague creases along the rim.

Sun and Fleece are the last to leave the room. They look up at Mayor Harrier and he shouts at them to stop.

'I suggest you stay away from that girl.'

Fleece speaks up first.

'She's OK Mayor Harrier, just a little upset that's all.'

'No, what she said about Victor Poodle can't be forgiven.'

Sun.

'She didn't mean anything by it Mayor.'

'She will not be allowed forgiveness.' (aggressive)

Mayor Harrier puts the bowler hat back on his head and walks out through the back of the stage.

lieutenant brett dachshund and bobby hound play cards in the provisional police hut

Victor Poodle built the perfect society. Plentiful resources and equality. He knew there was no real need to infuse a concept like crimininality into a place like New Luddle. But he also knew a little something about human behaviour. He knew human behaviour wasn't uniform. Replicative, yes, imitative, certainly, but not uniform. Societies like New Luddle appear to be strong, impenetrable walls of harmony and like-mindedness, but search hard enough, look closely and you see the little pixels, molecules jostling together, climbing on shoulders, crawling through legs, each one a tiny but distinct individual operating by itself. Working for others, yes, desiring the greater good, certainly, but make no mistake, they do so of their own will and they can change their mind anytime they like. Yeah, Victor Poddle knew a little something about people alright. He knew that some form of anomie ghosts around any society and that sometimes it takes shape and sometimes it doesn't. Most importantly, he knew the anomie ghost was there.

So Victor created the provisional police. The provisional police consists of a fully-trained lieutenant and a trainee lieutenant who is prepared for the job upon the retirement or death of the serving lieutenant. It is worth noting that the provisional police have no authority or power. They are inactive. (some Ludlows call them the 'sleeping police' although this is unfair as sitting in a hut all day playing cards is enough to make anybody tired.) Technically, there is no police force in New Luddle. However, should a crime be committed the provisional police will be activated and become the official police with the power to arrest and detain and bring persons to justice etcetera. Each lieutenant and trainee has an NLPD badge kept in a drawer in the police hut. They are to be taken out and worn only when the concept of crime introduces itself to New Luddle. Until that day, the only authority in New Luddle is the Mayor.

The present lieutenant is the dashing Brett Dachshund. He's been the lieutenant for ten years now and feels (despite the purported equality in New Luddle) that if you were to draw up some kind of hierarchy of New Luddle then he would be featuring somewhere near the top of the pyramid. A pretty important guy in other words. Secretly, he can't wait for the day he becomes officially instated as a bona fide police lieutenant instead of this provisional nonsense. Until that day he keeps himself occupied in his role as mentor and tutor. His trainee is Bobby Hound. A keen sleuth himself, Bobby may not be the brightest star in the sky (more dark matter) but he is always the first to ask a question. He's the sort of person who likes to know things. Although in fairness (irony) you couldn't say he knew a whole lot.

'Boss?'

'Yes Bobby.'

'Do you know something?'

'I know lots of things Bobby, put down a card will you eh?'

'Well, I heard that in Dupont they have thousands of real police officers walking the streets, solving crime - I mean like real crime, murders and stuff - all day every day.'

'I'm sure they do Bobby, the place is a mess. What's your point?'

'Eh?'

'What made you say it? Goodness me Bobby now where did you get that two of hearts from, give them here I'll deal this time.'

'Well, wouldn't you like to do that Boss, you know, solve crimes all day long, wouldn't that be better than playing gin rummy?'

'Goodness me Bobby, have I not taught you anything? Better than gin rummy? Crime all day long? Have you suddenly become twisted?'

'No.'

'Why do you think there's no crime in New Luddle, Bobby?'

'Because Victor Poodle built and nurtured a perfect society, Boss.'

'Well yes, there is that. But I'd say the chief reason is because of us.'

'Us?'

'Yes, us Bobby. The (potential) law enforcement agency that governs this colonies moral and ethical requirements. There's plenty of criminals in New Luddle alright.'

'There is?'

'Oh yeah, a cornucopia of crims in this colony.'

'But Boss?'

'Yeah?'

'How come they never commit any crime? I mean there has never been a crime committed here. What kind of criminals are we dealing with Boss?'

'Well, I'd say the clever kind, Bobby.'

'Clever? I think maybe they're just lazy Boss, you know what this sun can do to you.'

'(tut) They know not to commit any crime here because if they did, boy if they did (almost licks lips) ... you know what would happen don't you?.'

'What?'

'They'd be activating us Bobby. They'd be the ones to establish a real genuine N.L.P.D instead of this fiasco of a pretend type thing. We'd be on to them like a flash. And tell me Bobby, what kind of criminal brings about the existence of a police force when he or she (never forget the existence of women, Bobby) currently lives in a police-free criminal paradise?

'Not sure Boss. A burglar?'

'No, Bobby! Goodness me, I'm referring to the criminal's mentality, not their genre.'

'Oh, in that case a pretty stupid one Boss.'

'Correct, a pretty stupid one, and as I said before Bobby the countless criminals in New Luddle are all pretty clever because they know... Goodness me Bobby is that another two of hearts? Do you never shuffle these cards properly?'

And so on and so forth. The New Luddle Police Department. The NLPD sit, play cards, discuss the job and wait. Wait for the day they become legitimized, called into action, the day they've been training for all their lives. No more imagined simulation. No more daydreams of wrestling weapons to safety or acted-out interrogations. The day everything becomes real. For real. So they sit. And wait. The NLPD sit. And wait. And play cards.

*sun and fleece leave school and find daisy
in beth's café drowning her sorrows with a
cup of tea*

It is half past three and school is over. Sun and Fleece charge out
of the doors and exit the grounds through a five-bar wooden gate
that leads to a dust track at the side of the school. It takes longer
this way but they can be alone. It has not been a good day. Both
Sun and Fleece were distracted and paid little attention to the
Friday history lecture given by the beautiful Kelly Chihuahua. A
fine recounting of the events of 1924 and the portentous 'Sewing
Summer', as it became known, when a Gossypium (cotton) plant
was discovered by a tomato grower in the undergrowth. The
introduction of cotton revitalised New Luddle's staid fashion and
brought a much needed coolness and comfortability to the
Ludlows' clothing. Kelly Chihuahua described the events with
humour and accessibility without trivialising the historical shift
that took place during this remarkable summer of change. At one
point she described it as an 'epoch for the sock'. Her infectious,
homing intonation begot a response combining anticipation with
concentration, something not normally associated with history
lectures. Just about all the pupils were rapt and intrigued, all
except Sun Saluki and Fleece Dingo, who felt a certain
portentousness surrounding their own summer.

Daisy had always been opinionated and often rude but there
was something climactic about her behaviour right now. Like a
fuse fast running out of cord to practise on.

'Fleece I'm worried.'

'Don't be.'

'But I am. I really am.'

'You know how she is. How she's always been.'

'Yeah but not like this. She'll say that shit to us, but the Mayor? She's never spoken out like that before.'

'I know, and the way she just strolled out ... you realize she'll have been sat in Beth's café for the last six hours, don't you? Having one of their "special chats". What is it with them two?'

'Fuck knows. That's women, I guess.'

'Really?'

(laughter)

'No, not really but it's good to simplify.'

They carry on along the dust track that will eventually lead them to Victor Poodle (as all roads in New Luddle do). Then they can cut across to Beth's café. At last the sun is starting to calm down and the air, you can tell, is thinking about changing into something a little cooler for the evening. The sky, still in blue, seems to be further away now. It's late afternoon in New Luddle, the most beautiful part of the day. Not that these two are paying any attention to it.

'Fleece?'

'Yeah?'

'Do you think you understand her?'

'Who?'

'Daisy.'

'How do you mean?'

'I mean regardless of whether you agree with the stuff she comes out with, do you understand where she's coming from, do you get why she says it?'

'I don't know. I think so.'

'Just... I think it's important. As... friends I think it's important to understand.'

'Listen Sun, the way I see it, she's just bored. Bored and letting off a bit of steam.'

'Really?'

'Really.'

'That's it.'

'That's it.'

'That's not a little...'

'Hey, come on – it's good to simplify.'

They arrive at Beth's café. A few workers have returned from the fields and are sat outside. The workers say good afternoon to Sun and Fleece and tut when they are ignored. This is all the workers talk about for the next forty-five minutes. Sun and Fleece didn't mean to insult the workers they just didn't hear, it wasn't as the workers suggested, 'a sympton of youth', they are just focused on finding Daisy and making sure she is OK.

She is OK. Sat slumped on a creaky wooden chair, gently rocking back and forth. Parts of her hair have fallen into the various cups of tea that litter the table. Sun and Fleece see her and fill up with relief. She is OK. This is quite normal. She looks up.

'Hey, I was hoping you'd come and find me.'

Fleece pulls up a chair while Sun hurriedly asks questions, standing awkwardly, feeling stupid and too tall because everyone else in the café is sat down.

'How are you doing Daisy? We were worried ... how are you... holding up?'

'Holding up? What are you on about Sun – has someone died?'

'No I just mean... I don't know, fuck me Daisy you're in big trouble. Don't you see how much shit you're in?'

'No, I don't see myself in any shit. Look sit down will you Sun, you're making me tense.'

Sun sits down and the three of them order a cup of tea from Beth, who keeps pestering them about Sun's birthday, asking how they intend to celebrate. So far they have ignored her but she keeps coming back, which annoys Sun because he wants to talk to Daisy. He wants to make sure she really is OK. Not the casual everyone-saying-it-for-no-reason OK, but the OK that has actual meaning. He would like to be serious. Eventually, when the tea arrives, Dasiy wants to be serious too. She finally decides.

'I'd just had enough, you know?'

Daisy pulls back her hair. Her skin is very white and her eyes shot through with blood. Fallout from tears (long, galloping tears) have left blotches and stains ugly on her face.

Her body is loose and droopy like bits of muscle and flesh might slip off her bones. She looks drained, like her emotions have been sicked out. Looking at her now, she doesn't seem OK.

'Talk, Daisy,' Sun pleads.

She will. And. She does.

'This place and... him. I don't know. It's just so fucking content. So stupidly happy. It's dumb. It's really dumb. Nobody ever speaks.'

Fleece glances away, not really knowing what to say and not wanting to get too involved. Like Daisy he often wonders about New Luddle and how much of himself will never be discovered because of it. If truth be told, he gets a little scared by these thoughts. If truth be told, he prefers to look away and think of other things. Sometimes he finds this too hard and fails to come up with other things to think about. That's when he is most careful not to speak. But this is only if the truth be told.

Sun is intent. He moves his chair right up to Daisy's knees.

'What do you mean nobody speaks? Just tell it straight for once: what's the real problem here Daisy?'

She looks up at Sun. She stares into his face for a while, making a judgment, rotating her head, wondering just how much she really can tell. She looks at Sun to see what she has inside. She feels her guts move, they sliver and freeze in her stomach. Both shoulders sink. Not enough. She doesn't have enough inside.

'New Luddle. That's the problem Sun. Do you really not see it? Do you really think this is human beings, men and women at their very best?'

'Well, yeah I do actually. We work together, respect one another, we share our resources, ensure equality, never any crime, never any war. Essentially, we don't fight or covet. I say that's human beings at their best.'

Daisy shakes her head and drinks her tea. She tries to explain.

'Sorry Sun but that's bullshit. Where's the artist? The poet? The dreamer? The battling of minds, of ideas? The contrast, the opinion? Where? We're like braindead clones here. Where's the fucking human being in this place, Sun? Us at our best? It's discovering who we really are. Stretching ourselves, using every corner of our brain, speaking every word in our mind. Excitement, anger, curiosity, choice, fucking choice. This place is like an experiment, a blazing hot laboratory. It's not real. Victor Poodle wasn't any messiah, he was a social scientist who wanted to use us for a test case. To see what would happen. Right, let me see, we'll reduce their range of emotions, establish only one way of life, narrow their minds, convince them they're in heaven, and the result? They get on, they get on fine. They are happy, hurrah, it worked. Great, fascinating, but the truth is I don't really care all that much about getting on. It's all very nice and quaint this "one big happy family" but I'd be prepared to sacrifice it, I really would. I'd give it up. If it meant freedom to explore just what it is we are capable of doing, then I'd do it. If it meant an understanding of who we are as separate beings to one another, as independent souls, then I'd trade the ignorance and the safety. I'd trade it like that. Give me knowledge, give me a bit of danger any day. Then you'd have happiness, proper happiness, not the self-hypnotizing contentedness we have here.'

Sun slowly bangs his head on the table. Twice.

Dasiy is beaming, her face full of tiny, crinkled smiles. That good old slice of polemical oratory has perked her right up. Good to get these things off your chest. She waves an empty cup in the direction of Beth who nods and brings over a new pot.

Sun doesn't know what to think. The constant rants and raves seem to liberate and upset Daisy at the same time. One second she's empowered by a sense of radicalism and demand for free thought, the next she's crying into her tea over the lack of choice and variety in New Luddle life.

Sun respects her opinions and all but can't stand it when she's down, hates the sadness. The bitter fury. And he can't agree. I'm sorry, he says, but I can't agree. He tries to understand, to really grasp the essence of Daisy's views but he doesn't really see where she's coming from. How can you complain about New Luddle? It's ridiculous. She's completely overdoing this individual freedom bit for a start. Of course they're free. That's the point isn't it? They're free from war, free from selfishness, free from inequality. To have all these kinds of really big freedoms it seems entirely fair to sacrifice a little tiny piece of your own personal freedom in return. The way Sun figures, it's simple: if on the whole everyone is happy and content, then there isn't, on the whole, any reason not to be happy and content. Simple. He likes that. Simple. Like a slogan.

Fleece is glad to hear the conversation break from the deep and meaningful. Better to just live day by day, he thinks. Don't worry about the future, forget about the past. That's the way. He likes that. Don't worry about the future, forget about the past. Simple. Like a cop-out, he thinks. Like a nice yellowy cop-out. Forget everything. Think nothing. Huh. (self pity)

'So what did Mistress Feist say anyway?'

'You've gotta go meet with the Mayor on Sunday morning.'

'Just the two of us?'

'Yeah I guess.'

'I'm not meeting just the two of us.'(apprehension)

Daisy pushes her chair back and folds her arms over her chest.

Fleece leans forward stretching his elbows further along the table. He's back in the loop. Glad to be with friends again.

'I think it'll be OK, he'll have calmed down by then. Thought he was going to put a hole in that stupid hat though, the way he was twiddling it.'

They laugh. Sun lifts his head back.

'Oh yeah, we'd better go Fleece'

'Why? You've only been here a few minutes.'

'Because we're meant to stay away from you, Daisy Spaniel, you're bad news you are. Remember what the Mayor said, Fleece?.'

'Shit yeah, I almost forgot. Good advice I think. Sorry Daisy, we just don't want to be corrupted that's all.'

They stand to leave. Daisy has none of it.

'Yeah yeah. Fuck off.'(smiling)

They sit back down. (all smiling)

Beth comes out from the kitchen to clear away bits of the mess on the table.

'So Sun, you still haven't told me what you're doing tonight.'

'Tonight?'

'To celebrate. What is this? You're going to be celebrating your fifteenth birthday, right?'

They look at one another, then look away, then look back to one another. Sun realizes he's going to have to speak. They can't all just sit there moving their heads back and forth.

'Not sure yet Beth.'

'Not sure? (amazed) But Sun, in a couple of hours before you'll be wanting to come back out, heck it's gone five-thirty now!'

'Yeah, I s'pose it is getting on, don't worry, we'll think of something.'

'Well why don't you come back here I'll cook you up a nice...'

Sun interupts and is firm.

'Listen Beth, to be honest we had kind of organized something.'

'Well, why didn't you say so?'(confused)

'Because...

'What?'

'We're... well, you see...'

'This is ridiculous Sun, you've been avoiding the topic all afternoon, why can't you just tell me?'

'Because we're going over to Ned Corgi's.' (failure)

There is silence. Beth's face drops thirty feet below her heart, sinking in soil, rapidly burying itself. Hearing his name spoke by Sun somehow makes it worse. She wasn't that much older herself.

'That's great (-) you'll have fun(-) No really(-) that's great.'

Daisy can do nothing but allow tears to ride down her face again. She can't remember a day when so many fell down. Fleece can't bear to look up. Wishes he wasn't here, or at least not visible.

'Sorry Beth.'

'What for? I don't know why you'd be sorry... listen you...'

Beth's eyes have ensconced themselves in red pouches of skin. Already they are puffed up and bright red. They look like her speciality: tomatoes in pastry. Narrow blue veins form under her cheeks and push up to map the sorrow. She wipes her face with both hands and stands straight, maintaining a serenity that is hard-fought, getting hold of herself once more.

'...you say hi when you see him.( )Just... just say I said hello, alright?'

She turns and walks back into the kitchen. They hear leaden feet clatter each stair as she climbs up. They hear a door slam shut. They hear a cry. They hear nothing. They don't hear any sobs or a mirror smash on the floor. They stop hearing.

the story of ned corgi and beth pointer, two young lovers whose relationship started off well but ended badly

It has been commented upon many times that life for a New Ludlow is remarkably uncomplicated. And it's true. It follows three simple stages. Schooling to the age of fifteen. Work in the fields. Retirement at forty. No wonder they are content. But this three step formula doesn't apply to everyone. 'For any society to function effectively there needs to be some degree of flexibility in the labour market.' (Victor Poodle, of course.) So, in New Luddle there has and continues to be a small, disparate group of citizens who form a necessary but rare exception to the three-step rule. Generally speaking, those escapees of the three-step rule are the Mayor, teachers at the school, the priest and his assistant and the provisional police - all of whom lead very different and unique lives compared to other Ludlows. As does the very last exception - the café owner.

Third Mayor Rudyard Shih-tzu first introduced a café to New Luddle in the late 1940s. Mayor Shih-tzu was a forward thinking, progressive leader who implemented many new schemes and initiatives over his twenty-year tenure, each being met with a varied degree of success. The café is sadly the only remaining legacy of Mayor Shih-tzu's reign. The only one you could technically call a success (the only one to last beyond a week). The initial idea of opening a café was put forward by a fiery young mother of one named Sally Pointer. She explained to Mayor Shih-tzu in no uncertain terms (*by shouting*), that people, particularly

4 0

workers, would benefit from somewhere to sit down after work, rest their weary legs, drink some tea, eat some cake, make one another laugh. She said that New Luddle would not only benefit from a café but it was positively crying out for one. Sally even suggested the thus far lack of café facility could be viewed as something resembling an outrage. She was certainly forceful and direct in her approach.

The Mayor, being a man of unique foresight, immediately saw how such an outlet would indeed benefit a community like New Luddle, providing them with sustenance and sociability. The vision was clear in his mind: plants and flowers covering the veranda, sweet smelling and bright; small groups chatting away, drinking tea, smiling, laughing. Yes, absolutely, why not, take it, it's yours.

Within a few days, what was once a quiet stretch of dust in the top left-hand corner of New Luddle had became a hubbub of people, laughing and eating, sitting at tables, enjoying each other's company, drinking tea, deciding they were very happy and mighty lucky.

When Sally's granddaughter was born everyone was relieved because they knew the café could remain in the family for another generation: Beth's café. It was destiny, it was fortune, it was all so pleasant and nice. The café became an institution within New Luddle and remains so today.

****

Ned Corgi was considered the best tomato grower in New Luddle history. Some say he could make the tomatoes laugh just by smiling, cause them to widen and ripen by whistling a favourite tune. Nobody's patch has ever been more fecund. Nobody's tomatoes have ever been redder or rounder or as juicy. The tomatoes in his patch weeped when he was sad and prayed when he was ill. There was nothing they wouldn't do for him. He was a charmer. A smoothie. The Tomato Lathario. Everyone knew he had something about him, an irresistibility. It made him very popular.

Most of the uncoupled women in New Luddle had their eyes on Ned. He was always being asked out for walks or for dinner by desirable ladies, almost every day. But to each woman that asked him he would reluctantly say no. It wasn't that he didn't find these women attractive – they all seemed very nice. But as far as Ned was concerned, there was only one particular uncoupled woman for him.

Of course he'd seen Beth in the café many times. He still remembers the first, second, third, fourth time their eyes met, but she didn't seem interested. He was in love. She just cleaned the table and brought more tea, she wouldn't speak to him or smile. Walking home from the café after a day in the fields was always the saddest part of the day. Inside the café he played it nice and easy of course, no staring or looking soppy. But the reality is, he'd have swapped all the love of his tomatoes and all those other women, just for a smile from Beth. Just for a smile. Walking home he'd always imagine it. Nothing more. Just a smile. It was his fantasy.

Many months passed and the situation didn't change much. Ned became so depressed that even the tomatoes seemed to take on a shade of concerned red. One Wednesday lunchtime, the workers went to the café for lunch. Ned decided he'd had enough, he couldn't face seeing Beth again, so he told the workers he would stay behind and continue working, that he wasn't at all hungry. For the following twenty minutes he engaged so fully with his work that for the first time in months all memory of Beth disappeared from his mind.

So, turning around after receiving a tap on the shoulder, it came as a shock to see her standing nervously, smiling (yes, smiling), a mug of hot tea in one hand, a small tomato cake in the other, saying: 'You can't not eat.'

Beth knew of Ned's reputation with the ladies and the tomatoes. She too loved him from the moment their eyes met but didn't for a second imagine Ned could feel the same. When he hadn't arrived with the others for lunch that Wednesday she just had to find him. She had to tell him how she felt. She didn't care how stupid or sad it might seem. All the time in the café she'd felt uncomfortable, scared to make a fool out of herself. Outside in the fields she was free and shivering with bravery.

Ned didn't drink the tea or eat the tomato cake. Instead he returned the smile and they held one another and kissed. Under the jealous eyes of a thousand tomatoes they kissed.

The romance continued for almost two years. They were together at every possible moment. They couldn't be without each other. But it wasn't a dependency. It was desire and want; not need, but a simple, beautiful, choice.

With this in mind, when you think how together, how conjoined their lives had become, it is hard to imagine how such a thing, such a potent loving unison, could fail. But fail it did. Perhaps the bond wasn't quite as strong as it first seemed. Perhaps love itself isn't that strong after all. Maybe it's brittle, maybe it's always just waiting to fall apart. Who's to say?

Then came another Wednesday afternoon just like the one two years previously.

Beth decided, as it was quiet in the café, to pop up to the fields with some cake and tea again, just as she had done two years ago. She could spend a few minutes with Ned, hopefully he would eat the cake and drink the tea this time. It would be a nice surprise. She was eager to see Ned's reaction, his pleased face. She was glad to have thought of it.

Walking across one of the fields Beth could see Ned crouched down with a few of the workers around him. She called out. Some of the workers looked back and waved. Ned didn't move. She called again but Ned made no movement, he was just stood there with his back turned, hunched over, perfectly still. She called again three times. Nothing. Beth began to panic. She was too close for him not be able to hear. Why was he ignoring her? Had she upset him? Hopeless ideas gained legs and began pacing furiously in her mind. Maybe he'd stopped loving her? Maybe he was embarrassed by her. This time she screamed, panicking and angry, she screamed for Ned to turn around. And this time he did turn around.

And the sledgehammer came down towards the stake he should have been holding in place.

And it smashed his hand, shattering bones, splicing two fingers straight off, severing a third. Knuckles switched places with each other, his wrist split, freeing narrow lines of blood to spring frantically from open veins.

And Beth could see the red liquid ejaculate high into the air, crazily spraying red everywhere, in workers' clothes and faces, eyes and mouths.

And she ran, not towards Ned, not to help, but she ran. She ran up and back and across the colony, her direction as skewed as the blood fleeing Ned's arm.

And she wasn't sure what to do.

And she wasn't sure what she'd done.

It was of course a tragic accident. Beth shouldn't have got so paranoid and upset, screaming at Ned like that. Ned shouldn't have turned around when he did. He should have just waited and explained afterwards. He tried desperately to stay still and focused, but hearing Beth like that, he had to turn to her.

But you wouldn't want to apportion any blame in these sorts of scenarios – it was a tragic accident, a blameless incident. And nobody did. Except Ned. Except Beth. And the trouble with physical trauma is that there's always a scar, a visible reminder, an immediate association. In Ned's case it's a wooden hand. Beautifully carved by a couple of the tree men, Ned wears it freely, no glove, no shame. The varnish coat is especially protective; in theory, it should last him forever. Everything that happened that day will last in him forever.

In the years that have passed Beth and Ned have spoken on occasion but neither one can bear to look in the other's eyes for fear of what might happen. The blame has dislodged itself fully from both their minds. Just sadness remains. It would seem that Ned's wooden hand means their relationship is over - or, it should be said, the accident resulting in Ned's wooden hand means their relationship is over. Love must be brittle. Always ready to snap.

****

Life for Beth, after the accident, remained constant. She's never had a relationship with anyone else and not many believe she ever will, but working in the café has kept her busy and she seems happy most of the time.

Ned on the other hand, Ned's life has changed immensely. For some reason, perhaps prejudice, a judgment of some kind, nobody knows, the tomatoes stopped responding to Ned and his new wooden hand. They were steadfast in their refusal to grow or reproduce. Ned, like everyone else, couldn't understand this reaction. He was still the same person after all. But obviously the tomatoes didn't see it that way: for them, everything had changed.

A few weeks of failed work in the fields and Ned was granted an absence break of six months. The longest in New Luddle history. It was thought a rest and some time away would benefit Ned and his tomatoes. In absence he became something of a recluse. Both Ned and Beth for a long time were the gust behind many whispers but while Beth faced up to them with her work in the café, the same couldn't be said for Ned. Not feeling able to go to the café ever again he developed a new life of self-dependency. He quickly realized after a few days of starvation that he would need to learn how to cook. And fast. This in itself was depressing for Ned as, like most of the residents, he was so used to the taste of food prepared by Beth that he couldn't imagine anything being as good. How could he make tomato cake and then expect to eat it without thinking of her? Eat it without crying?

So instead he began to experiment. To begin with the disasters outweighed the successes. He worked out that it was a remarkable ratio of eighteen to one. But it didn't take too long before the ratio began reversing itself and after a few months Ned found he could easily produce delicious dishes carved from wholly original recipes. All by himself.

Ned's wooden hand was understandably awkward and cumbersome to deal with at the start. But Ned realized that he might be able to utilize it in his cooking and it has now become a major asset in the kitchen. Being able to withstand practically any heat, he uses it to mix his famous tomato sauces. It operates as a gauge. He knows a sauce is ready once the varnish on his hand turns a particular shade of red. This is also how each sauce acquires its name, the most popular being Classic Crimson and Vintage Vermillion. This is contestable though as the recent addition of Tasty Terracotta to the menu may have upset the established favourites at the top of the taste polls.

Being the man Ned is, it didn't take too long before he felt ready to breathe in New Luddle's socially oxygenated atmosphere once more. Still avoiding Beth and the café, he began inviting people round to his house for evening meals. His culinary repertoire expanding daily, the self-titled 'Ned's Night' was a roaring success. It restored a lot of personal confidence in Ned and gave him an excellent platform to show off his unique, self-acquired skill of tomato blended cooking. Ned delighted his fellow colonists with sweet tastes and exuberant flavours. Nobody had ever tasted anything like the food Ned was producing. Previously the people of New Luddle had just eaten basic tomato recipes served as cake or in pastry. It filled them up and tasted pretty good, which was all they wanted. But now they found with Ned's

Night they were eating for pleasure, for the experience. Ned, by himself, commanded only by his individual will, had produced something new and beautiful.

But of course all of this was still unofficial. Before long Ned's six-month absence break was up and he returned to the fields. His tomatoes still refused to grow. It would appear tomatoes can hold a substantial grudge. Ned felt that perhaps they had been spoilt and this selfish attitude was the result. A lesson in parenting maybe.

Ned's Night continued but with diminished frequency. Ned refused to keep the same menu for more than a week but found he didn't have the time, now that he was back in the fields, to invent new recipes. This caused great frustration in the colony. The New Ludlows didn't want to wait a whole month before tasting Succulent Scarlet or Piquant Poppy sauce. They wanted it now. Eventually Ned decided he'd had enough. His work in the fields was still proving unproductive, he found the tomatoes were being contrary to the point of sheer bloody-mindedness, yet he was simultaneously providing a restricted yet highly successful service with Ned's Night. It didn't seem right. Wouldn't New Luddle benefit more if he left the fields and just concentrated on cooking permanently? Nobody would mind, in fact he had the backing of the people. He decided to go to the Mayor. Mayor Cudrip Harrier himself. He even wrote out a small business proposal using graphs and scattergrams to show projected growth and productivity levels based on demand and competition. Ned felt his projections were accurate and very attractive. Plus, if you can have a Beth's café why not a Ned's Night?

To begin with Mayor Harrier was confused. He read the situation quite simply. Ned had lost his touch with the tomatoes, decided he prefered cooking instead and so felt it OK to break with ethical tradition and utilitarian principle to become an entrepeneur. The very thing New Luddle was against - selfish economic endeavour.

'I've every right to ridicule. Have you forgotten our utilitarian principles or do you just not care?' is what he said.

But ahh, Ned argued, this *is* utilitarianism, as it's for the greater good. More people will be happy as a result.

But it's not fair, it's not right, the Mayor replied. What would Victor Poodle say? You can't just decide you're bored with working in the fields and set up on your own, based on a whim. What if more of us started doing that eh? What if Ferry Doberman decided he wasn't fussed about working in the fields anymore and wanted to be a full-time runner? Should I grant him that too? Should we all just stop working in the fields and find ourselves a hobby? The great strength of this society is a conformity to selflessness. When we start to behave for the benefit of ourselves alone, this place starts to crack until eventually it splits open. I can't let you be the first splinter Ned. I'm not Mayor Shih-tzu. I won't bow down to this pressure.

Ned hadn't predicted Mayor Harrier would be so hardline in his response. The savvy proposal and growth-related forecast didn't move him a bit. It was clear the scatter graphs and pie charts weren't going to be of any benefit. To make matters worse, the more Ned campaigned to the Mayor, the more he talked about Ned's Night and all it's possibilities, the more his desire increased. He wasn't going back to the fields. He'd made up his mind. He didn't care. He wanted Ned's Night more than anything.

In one final act of desperation Ned invited the Mayor for a private tasting session at his house. He would show the Mayor just how spectacular his talent was. Under the spell of a Vintage Vermillion the Mayor would surely say yes to anything. After much grumbling, the Mayor agreed to the tasting session. He should, he supposed, see what all the fuss was about.

Nobody is quite sure just what went on that night. Some say it was the Ravishing Ruby that swung it, others put it down to a large helping of Classic Crimson. But whatever the sauce it's always been assumed that Mayor Harrier was bowled over by the food he tasted because within the week Ned's house had been converted into a nice little restaurant called Ned's Night and the proprietor, Ned Corgi, couldn't have been happier with his new life. Bookings weeks in advance, happy faces, delicious food – it was, predictably, a roaring success from the opening night onwards. It truly was a new life for Ned, the new life he'd demanded. The new life he'd have given anything for. He could get on now with thinking less about Beth Pointer and more about himself, and his recipes.

And while all this was going on Beth continued working assiduously. She didn't speak to anyone about the newly established Ned's Night, just carried on as normal. Happy that Ned had started again, happy for him. Happy for her broken other.

sun saluki celebrates his fifteenth birthday with daisy spaniel and fleece dingo at ned corgi's famous restaurant ned's night

PART ONE: Unexpected behaviour

'You enjoy yourself now Sun.'

'Yeah, will do mum.'

'You have a good time.'

'Sure.'

'You take care.'

'I'm going now mum. I'll probably be late back.'

'Why?'

'What do you mean why? It's my birthday night. My fifteenth. It'll be a late night.'

'I know, I know, it's just that a mother worries Sun that's all. What do you call late?'

'Mum, this is New Luddle, remember. What's there to worry about? I'll be late. It'll be fine.'

'OK. Well try not to wake anyone then. Least of all me.'

'Sure mum.'

'You take care.'

'See you in the morning.'

'Have a good night... love you.'

'Yeah, you too.'

Sun Saluki steps out of his house and makes his way to Ned Corgi's. The air is cool and comfortable. Today marks the end of an era. Next year, Sun will celebrate his birthday having worked all day in the fields, providing for his community. It feels a bit weird to him. Weird that it should happen so soon. It's the right thing of course, it's what everyone does. It's always been this way and it's proven to work but still, he can't help but feel anxious about the whole thing. Something is niggling him. He isn't sure what. More than anything it seems to be the age thing. He is fifteen now and so, technically speaking, a man. This is why he must leave school and work in the fields. But I don't feel like a man, thinks Sun. I don't feel like I have any kind of knowledge of anything. Me, Daisy and Fleece, we're just kids. There must be loads of stuff we don't know yet, life stuff. I suppose I just don't feel ready, that's what's bugging me, I feel a little bit young to be starting my job for life, the next twenty-five years slaving away in a field. Maybe it doesn't feel right because it isn't right, being made to finish school, being told your job, maybe... no hang on I'm starting to sound like Daisy. This is New Luddle, this is perfect, it's always been this way, forget about it. It's a good system, the best – it must be the right thing. This is New Luddle. We're all happy here, what am I worrying about? He remembers a slogan from the bumper of a Dupontian car:

Buy. Eat. Crap. Sleep. Living life Dupontian style!

You couldn't say its meaning was crystal clear in Sun's mind but he thinks there is a message there and probably a valuable and truthful message too. That life is not a complicated or difficult process but a simple one, and we shouldn't forget that. Remembering this slogan brings comfort to Sun. Why is he trying to complicate things? He blames Daisy. Then he smiles. He'll see her soon. And working in the fields will be fine. It's good to give something back. This is how it's always been. It's perfect. Everyone knows it's perfect. There is nothing wrong. They are the lucky ones.

Sun Saluki playfully kicks up dust and jogs the rest of the way to Ned Corgi's. Happier now. A lot happier.

It is a Friday night which almost certainly means a full house at Ned's Night. This is good because it creates a wonderful lively atmosphere and bad because Ned is the only cook, and being the only waiter too, it takes a very long time to order your food and eat. The residents are so happy though, it doesn't matter a jot. Sun, Daisy and Fleece booked their table weeks ago. It was the only one left. Right next to the kitchen door. It's known to be the worst table as Ned crashes in and out, clattering pots and pans. They don't care. Table placing isn't something they think about.

When Sun arrives it is six forty-five and already Ned is sweating and panicked, but he still finds time to hug Sun and congratulate him on turning fifteen. Sun laughs and makes a joke about how it really wasn't that hard a thing to do and Ned Corgi smiles, not really understanding, and dusts Sun's hair mockingly.

Daisy is sat down at their table. She has been sat down for almost twenty minutes. Hair covers her face but is pushed away when she sees Sun. Before he even sees her in the corner, she is smiling at him. She waves. He reaches her and they hug. They hold each other longer than usual and for the first time kiss one another on the lips. It is brief and unrehearsed but nevertheless Daisy and Sun kiss. It comes as a shock to both of them.

Warm spots appear on their cheeks. Little bits glow inside. They hover a while and touch hands, they feel new and a bit different.

Daisy cannot stop smiling, she ties her hair back fully with an elastic band. She wants Sun to always see her face now.

Sun is shaking a little. It was unexpected, in his mind he was thinking about one day holding hands, just grabbing her hand as they walked, he was hoping to find the nerve to do that, but now this. He feels like he might just have learnt some of that life stuff he was thinking about on the way, learnt it in a couple of seconds. Maybe he is a man after all.

They sit down. Attempt composure. Stay quiet for a while.

It was brief and unrehearsed but nevertheless Daisy and Sun kissed.

Fleece walks in. He looks at Ned who is carrying three plates of Vintage Vermillion to table four. Ned smiles and does the best he can to gesticulate Sun and Daisy's position by the kitchen door. Fleece laughs a little. He sees where they are sat and makes his way over. He stops before sitting down.

'This is strange.'

'What?'

'I don't know.'

(awkwardness and quiet)

'That's great Fleece, do you wanna sit down or are you gonna stand there contemplating?'

'I will sit, thank you Daisy, I just felt a little alteration in the atmosphere that's all. Is there something going on I should know about?'

'No. Nothing.' (glow spots still on cheeks)

'OK?'

'Yeah OK, you both look pleased with yourselves that's all, it's very... furtive.'

'It's Sun's birthday. We're all happy. No secrets. Fuck me Fleece your imagination is... vivid.'

Daisy looks to Sun and winks. Sun smiles back. He is blushing. He is happy. They order a combination of small dishes from Ned who hides his annoyance that the fiddliest, most time-consuming dishes on the menu are being ordered at the busiest time of the busiest night, with a wide smile and suspicious giggle.

'No problem, I'll bring them out as quick as I can.' (flustered)

'Thanks Ned.'

There is a thoughtful silence before Sun explains his concerned face.

'It'll take him ages. I feel bad.'

'Fuck it. It's your birthday Sun. Enjoy it.'

'Daisy's right Sun. Fuck it. It's your birthday – field boy.'

They laugh but then Sun has to remind himself about those earlier thoughts on becoming 'field boy' and how his conclusion was that there is nothing wrong, in a few months he would be in the fields, older, wiser and prepared, and that would be fine. Nothing is wrong with that. He felt he had to remind himself.

It takes ages before Ned comes back. When he eventually arrives he is fully plated with three dishes in the wooden hand alone.

'Thanks Ned.'

'Sorry it took so long Sun, it's busy a night. You have a good birthday meal. There's a little something special in there but I'm not to tell, no one, to be done all, alone only secret...'

Ned gives his head a furious rub and dashes back to the kitchen, mumbling all the way, mopping his brow of sweat.

'Thanks Ned.' (jointly concerned)

'What was that about?'

'Ah nothing I don't think, you know how he is, he always talks weird when he's stressed out – it's like an affliction or something.'

'Yeah but Sun, never like that. He usually gets a few words jumbled up but that was different, that was all a bit delirious, don't you think? Did you hear what he was saying - there's something special in there? It's all a secret? I'm sorry but...weird. You'll agree with me Daisy won't you?'

'It was a bit odd, I don't know... maybe Sun's stew is poisoned, or something.'

They all laugh. Sort of.

The subject of Ned is pretty much dropped straight away. If it is an affliction in his speech then they all agree it is unfortunate and not something to be gossiped about. That would be wrong. And none of them believe that's what it is anyway.

Since the accident, and since Beth, it would appear that Ned Corgi's life has gone pretty well, but dip your head below the surface and you'll find this isn't the case. Open your eyes, look through the murky fluids and you'll see - it's when he is thinking of her. That's when the words get a little jumbled up. That's when everything gets confused. When he remembers her. It is an affliction. It is memory. She does it. Beth stops him from speaking properly. Stops him from functioning. She floods his brain. And there is nothing he can do. Except ease the pain. Ease the pain. Because it's not like it's ever going to stop.

It is a classic evening at Ned's Night. All the New Ludlows quietly eat their food, complimenting Ned at every possible moment. They talk about all sorts of things. Sun, Daisy and Fleece listen. It makes them laugh. One table discuss the fine crop of tomatoes this year and just how incomparable they are in terms of sweetness to those they were eating ten years ago. Another table, a bit further away, nearer the entrance, can't believe how hot it has been today, they say that God must have been in a particularly good mood when he awoke this morning. Near to them, on the table behind, a couple look rather sheepish as they talk about Ferry Doberman and how he might enter a marathon in Dupont. Neither thinks it a good idea. They think he should do the race in New Luddle because even if nobody else entered, which of course they wouldn't, it would still be a race, he'd still be running a marathon. Why does he need to go over there?

Daisy grins.

'You've gotta admire the logic, the way New Ludlows really understand situations. How they grasp the fundamentals of life. The human condition. It's pure... what do you call it... empathy.'

'Don't start Daisy. It's my birthday and that means you aren't allowed to spout any of your "look at me I'm such a rebel" anti-Luddle crap. Right Fleece?'

(smiling)

'Right, or me and Sun will hang you for treason.'

They all giggle.

'Yeah? You two couldn't hang a picture.'

(laughter)

'Right that's it... I'm ordering a tomato cake.'

'NED!' (group shout).

PART TWO: And again, but later on

The New Ludlows have gone home. Gone to sleep in their wooden houses after a last cup of tea on the verandha, with the smell of flowers hanging in the air and dusty shoes left sitting in the porch. Their stomachs filled and their hearts at rest. As if anything could be more pleasant.

Daisy, Fleece and Sun sit at their table in Ned Corgi's finishing cake. They have been the only ones left for half an hour now. Thinking back, they have been quite rowdy this evening, Daisy picking up (with glee) on all the 'off' looks they have received from fellow dining guests on nearby tables. It must have been the laughter, and the singing. Fleece in particular is a very bad singer. And the loudest. Since their after-dinner tea and tomato though, things have quietened down, and everyone has left. Except them.

'NED! (group shout)'

'... (silence)'

Since waving farewell to the last table of New Ludlows, Ned Corgi has yet to come out from his kitchen. Normally, Ned would come and sit with them, have a chat. Instead Fleece, Sun and Daisy just sit at their table, finishing cake, intermitently calling for Ned.

'Where is he?'

'What if something's happened?'

'Like what, Fleece?'

'I don't know. Probably nothing.'

Sun stands up. Daisy and Fleece continue.

'Well then, leave him alone, he probably just can't be doing with a big long midnight chat with us lot. He'll be in bed... it's church in the morning. Sun, what are you doing?'

Sun walks over to the kitchen door catching the corner of a table with his thigh on the way.

'Ow, my legs have gone a bit funny.'

'Where are you going?'

'Must have been sat down too long.'

'Sun?' (annoyed)

'I'm going to see if he's OK.'

'Don't worry about it, Daisy's right Sun, he'll be fine, probably in bed. Let's just finish the cake and go.'

'Yeah, come and sit down, we'll just go.'

'He would have said goodbye.'

'So he forgot, he's probably knackered.'

'Bollocks, he would definitely have cleared our plates before going to bed. I just want to check that's all. You two stay and finish the cake.'

'Alright, I can't be bothered to move right now anyway.'

'Yeah, alright we'll wait, but he'll pissed off if you wake him.'

Sun Saluki wouldn't normally bother with any of this mischief. He isn't the type. Normally, he'd be the one suggesting they sneak off home and leave Ned to it. Anything to avoid bother. For some reason though, maybe it's tied in with this whole coming of age phenomena he's been going through, maybe not, but for some reason, tonight his heart beats that little bit harder. He isn't quite so self-conscious. He feels loose and at ease, perhaps even a little adventurous. It's strange, something has gotten hold of him. Maybe this is really what happens when you turn fifteen – you change. You act differently, your character becomes different. Maybe this is what adulthood feels like. Sun rubs his leg, his balance is still unsteady. He isn't doing anything wrong. He just wants to see that Ned Corgi is OK.

He opens the kitchen door. The smell of tomatoes is sweet. There are pans and various types of red sauces everywhere. Sun closes the door behind him and ventures in further. The whole room is in a right state. There is no sign of Ned. It had never occurred to Sun before, just how much mess a night of cooking could make. Turns out it's a lot. Ned never has time to clean up as he goes along so he saves it all till the end. Sun thinks about all those times Ned has come and sat with them, talking till the early hours, never hurrying them out, all the time knowing he has a kitchen with mountainous plates and pans, stacked and filthy, still needing to be cleaned. Sun feels bad and a little shameful. Next time he will offer to help. Yes, he'll definitely do that, they can all help, Daisy and Fleece too, they won't mind. It would be good to do Ned a favour. Yes, decided, it's definite. That's what'll happen next time.

In the far corner of the kitchen, near the back door, alongside the various cups and bags of tomato skins, there is something strange. A pile of boxes, sealed and neatly stacked, jut out to fill what must be a quarter of the room. There are loads of them piled high on top of each other. Sun, led by his newly formed adventurous character trait, moves over and takes one of the boxes from the top of the pile. Without care (most unusual) he tears the seal and opens the lid of the box. Inside are round tubs each with identical labels – 'Ned's tomato soup'. Sun opens another box and finds the contents to be exactly the same. It's odd because Sun wasn't aware Ned did a tomato soup. He'd never seen it on the menu yet there was enough of the stuff in these boxes to feed the colony twice over. Sun felt confused and his head had started to hurt a little. It must be a new recipe or something. Anyway. He had gotten sidetracked. What Ned Corgi made and stored in his kitchen was of no concern to him. He was meant to be finding out where Ned had got to, not how his storage system worked, no matter how strange. He shouldn't have just opened the boxes like that. That was bad. It was rude. It wasn't very... Ludlow of him.

Sun decides to leave the kitchen as there is no sign of Ned. As he turns, banging his leg yet again, just below the knee this time, on a box filled with never-before-heard-of soup, he hears a vague cry coming from outside the back door. He quickly moves over and opens the door. Ned Corgi is sat on the steps. There are tears in his eyes and a bottle of whiskey in his hand.

'Ned... Ned are you OK? We were worried.'

'Damn it, sorry Sun, fuck, you shouldn't see me like this, no one should. That was the deal, fuck, sorry Sun.'

'What deal? Ned what's happened? What are you drinking? Shit, is that liquor?'

Sun sits down on the steps next to Ned. The top half of Ned's face looks red and bruised from tears and the strain of wretching. The bottom half is covered in black stubble. His eyes look only fractionally open.

There is a small pool of vomit on the last step. It drips down onto the ground like it's melting, except it's cold now. Everywhere is cold. The smell of it bobs in and around Sun's face. It is contagious and sweet but Sun refuses the temptation to gag.

'I'm sorry Sun, it just helps, you know?'

Sun tries to look compassionate but doesn't think it's worked. He feels dizzy.

'No, no you don't know it's all got just a bit... a bit... (coughing and tears)... a bit fucked up. Just totally fucking... (nothing) the drink helps me, he was right, it helps me... or it did... I'm just tired Sun (laughs) Tired and fucked.'

'Why, Ned? I don't understand, what's going on? Where are you getting this fucking liquor from... it's like a proper crime. There isn't meant to be any crime, Ned I don't understand... how?'

'It doesn't matter, please Sun, go, it doesn't matter, nothing matters, I'm sorry, this is bad, nobody was meant to... look I'm sorry...'

'Don't keep saying sorry Ned, I wanna help but I don't really understand...'

'I put it in your stew, I'm sorry.'

'What?'

'The whiskey. I put some in your stew, with your birthday and all I thought... I don't know, I wasn't thinking. I'm sorry Sun, real sorry I'm just a bit fucked, you'd better go, please don't tell anyone, about the liquor, please just forget, try and forget it all.'

'But Ned..'

'Please just go Sun, just go, just...'

Sick explodes from Ned's mouth again. It is red from the tomatoes and gooey. It drips down the wooden steps – a waterfall of blood and guts. The smell is again contagious and sweet and this time overcomes Sun. That whiskey-infused variety of tomato dishes, that only hours ago had been cooked to perfection and eaten with such relish, rise up from the pit of his stomach with speed, accelerating through the oesophagus and pharynx they burst out through his mouth like it's a crack in a dam wall. The force and violence of the reaction brings Sun to his knees. He spits and coughs until the pathways are clear. He stands.

'I'm gonna go now Ned, I really want to just... go.'

the story of religion and new luddle and
how it all came to be how it is today

Every Saturday morning the residents of New Luddle go to church. The St Bernard Church for Pentecostal Pantheists. It is a unique religion and one held dear by the older Ludlows. The arrival of pantheistic belief came pretty soon after the colony was formed. People were so heady with joy at their new surroundings (remember, these are people who had previously lived on what was essentially an iceberg) they immediately latched on to a 'God within nature' thread of belief and sowed it into a nice little religion. Of course, as you would expect, Victor Poodle was at the heart of an initial desecuralizing process, seeing it as something that could only be a positive for the colony and a natural companion to this new bucolic existence. Churchgoing was like farming or cups of tea - an essential for the country community. It didn't take long for an edifice to be erected and a font to be filled with the very best tomato juice.

The selection of a Pastoral was an easy process. Seeing as God was situated within the physical world around them, they would let *Him* decide. Various men put themselves forward. Each was requested to visit a fledgling tomato plant. They were asked to speak to the plant, caressing it if they chose, offer spiritual guidance and religious teaching. The plant that grew to hold the ripest, most perfect tomatoes would of course have been cared and instructed by that person chosen by God to be head the church of New Luddle. It was perfect and definitely fair, devised of course by the saviour himself- Victor Poodle.

The first ever Pastoral of New Luddle was a nice man called Father Mastiff. Trouble was, he had very little to work with, no bible, no perfunctory routines, no guidelines, no blueprint. Who knew when to genuflect, when to stand, sit, join in, keep quiet? Certainly not Father Mastiff. When starting off in an invented religion it's very much a case of ad lib to begin with (the lesson learnt). Fortunately, Father Mastiff was a pretty good ad libber. One of the best in fact. His improvised metaphors and analogies were so convincing that, as with any good religion, they soon, with a bit of time, became truth. They became the belief. The guideline, the blueprint.

'And God is watching us. Because he is all around. He is everywhere. And he can see us. All of us. With his eyes. His many eyes because each one of those tomatoes out there, each and every one of those are his eyes. Those are God's eyes people. He is watching us.'

Father Mastiff, Sermon 5, somewhere near the end.

This 'tomatoes being God's many eyes, always watching them', at some point stopped being an inspirational and guiding metaphor and became a kind of transcendental truth that Ludlows actually believed. Only after years and years and after the religion was so cemented into the colony's consciousness that it could never be ousted, did the odd young Ludlow begin to ask questions like, 'hang on, isn't that just a metaphor, the tomatoes on the plants aren't actually God's eyes are they? I mean not really.' Some replied, 'actually yes, they are actually God's eyes, so you had better watch out young man.' Others said 'no, of course they're not actually God's eyes, but the process of transubstantiation would make them God's eyes, so in effect they could be God's eyes if you think about it.' While some of the old sages of New Luddle would say, 'it is not for us to understand, but for him to tell us.'

Once, a youngster asked the naïve question, 'Why do we boil God's eyes in water and make cakes out of them, if they are... God's eyes, rather than tomatoes?' After the initial laughter had stopped a rather long silence occurred. Father Mastiff stepped forward. He was coming to the end of his tenure and was by now a very old man. He'd been the Pastoral for over fifty years. With a reassuring smile, he explained that the tomtoes do of course stop being God's eyes when they are picked from the plant: this is his gift to us. Everybody immediately nodded in agreement, breathed a sigh of relief and stared at the boy they felt had been made to look foolish.

And they believed it too. Even Father Mastiff, who had by this late stage in his life completely forgotten that it was only ever a piece of inspired improvisation that put the suggestion into people's minds in the first place. Genius really. It will survive forever.

And so things carried on. Crosses made from fruit, tomatoes carried by children at offertory and a general consistency of hurried sermons not fought by the congregation who had by now let the personal importance of mere attendance and routine take over from any real desire for religious teaching. So, as you can see, The St Bernard Church for Pantheists became just like any other church. Well, sort of. Until the present incumbent had his little revelation. Yes, Father Lurcher changed everything. What with his gift and all.

It all cracked off about twenty years ago now. The day of Father Lurcher's inauguration as the new Pastoral. The traditional selection process had been adhered to. Four men had put their names down and been given their fledgling tomato plant two months previously. Techniques varied. Two of the men shyly whispered to their plants, not wanting to overbear them, quiet encouragement was felt to be best. One man gave a slight caress just at the bottom of each tomato each day and a tickle under the leaves of the plant twice a week.

But Father Lurcher. Father Lurcher. Wow. His plant received a vibrant seminar in life coaching. Father Lurcher, or Brolly Lurcher as he was then, a confident man, was on top form, jumping up and down, punching the air, full of bravado and powerful persuasive technique. He managed to tap into and coax out an iron-like inner strength and instil a previously unknown confidence in his plant. By the end of the two months his plant was totally pumped and, as it repeated to itself over and over, it was 'ready to turn the opposition into juice'. Brolly Lurcher had made it clear to the plant that he didn't associate himself with losers, not ever, and now this was something they shared in common. They were both loser-free zones. In the end there was no contest. It was a stunning victory. As Father Lurcher said at the time, on numerous occasions, 'I'm so filled with God, oh I'm so filled with God, I bleed God, I feel him inside. Those other three? They're empty, empty vessels yeah? He's on board with me, he's on the deck with me, oh yeah.' A modest response from Brolly, who by now had become Father Lurcher. Chosen by God. He had been chosen by God.

And he was right. Apparently. God made his decision, he made the tomato plant trained by Father Lurcher grow to produce the finest tomatoes of the four plants.

Standing there, before the result had even been announced to an expectant crowd in front of Victor Poodle's statue, his face moved up and down in a continuous nodding gesture to denote a knowledge of his own victory. He shuffled his feet making a gravelly noise because of the sand. And once Mayor Cudrip Harrier made the announcement, Father Lurcher raised his arms to the sky, still nodding furiously, saying just two words, 'oh yeah, oh yeah'. It felt as though there should have been some sort of trophy handed out to commemorate the event. An oversized heavy belt perhaps. Mayor Harrier lifted his bowler hat to signify congratulations. And that was that. Father Lurcher. The champion elect. Chosen by God, no less. He knew it. Knew he was special. That smile. Milky white, glow-in-the-dark teeth, blond hair reflecting the morning sun. This was his day. Oh yeah. He stepped forward to acknowledge the clapping hands of all the residents. It was the least humble, least dignified acceptance from a Pastoral in the history of New Luddle. And still all Father Lurcher could bring himself to say (in aggressive, punchy tone) was: oh yeah.

In accordance with tradition, the final appendage to the inaugral ceremony, before the Mayor walks the new Pastoral to the church, is an introductory sermon. A bit like an acceptance speech. The new incumbent usually lays out their unique vision of Pantheism for New Luddle which generally tends to be notable only for its remarkable similarity to the previous incumbents' unique vision of Pantheism for New Luddle. Father Lurcher's was slightly different though.

> *Chosen by God. Me. Me. I knew it. I knew it. He's inside me. No wait. We're the same. Yes, we're the same, me, God we're one, I am he, he is me, I am … no, but he is in me, he fills me, the Spirit, I have the spirit, it is me. It's me.*

These are the thoughts of Father Lurcher as he stands in silence looking to the sky. He is overcome. It has all caught up with him – the day, the achievement, the so very clear victory. He's struggling to make sense of it all. His body feels light and tingly. He has been chosen by God. By Him. It explains everything. He knew he was amazing. Knew it. And now he finally knows why. This incredible realization entrances Father Lurcher, puts him under some kind of zombie spell. His arms reach out. His mind now a cloud of dreams, the images confused, tangled, blurred.

And still the crowd await.

And when he does finally speak, it goes like this:

'I am he, the spirit and I speak to tou (pause) I say... (near faint) it is better ter ter (head swimming, tingly body) thaf ff ker ker eryitus (struggling, wobbling) wib woberry fewton m(filled with God, of course, knew it had to be something like that) mm zoop rayyy de rayyyyyyy dedede(why he is so amazing) rigxs lep ton mukwerzel dost mendieta (long pause) I speak.' (gone) (collapse) (flat on back)

A baffled crowd rushed to Father Lurcher. A woman took him in her arms and called for water and a damp cloth. The woman nursed the unconscious Father Lurcher for about ten minutes, gently dabbing his head and rocking him back and forth. That's all it took to bring him back. Ten minutes of holding his head, moving a damp cloth on and off his forehead. The woman had stepped forward. She had volunteered.

But while Father Lurcher lay lifeless, in the kind woman's arms, the gathered colony didn't really know what to make of it all. They struggled for an explanation. Obviously this man was special. He had definitely been selected by God to be their spiritual counsellor. There was no refuting that. But to those stood there, listening to the undecipherable sermon, it would appear he was also definitely insane. It was a difficult and confusing task, trying to match up these two conflicting observations. To the humble Ludlow it didn't seem to make much sense having an insane man as the colony's spiritual counsellor. But it was God's decision, he wouldn't have made such a mistake, surely. Not God of all people. And if He thought it OK then that's that, but a strange choice all the same. Yes, whispered someone, but we know of course that God is a maverick! Too true, roared a listener-in, he has something in mind for us, you can be sure of that.

This was the point at which Mayor Cudrip Harrier stepped forward to inform the colony just what God did have in mind.

'Please, please, calm your anxiety. I have been listening to the discussions taking place, I have heard argument and counter-argument but let me tell you, I have wonderful news. What you just witnessed was a miracle.'

Gasps and cries and one instinctive shout of 'Really?'

Yes really, young man. As you can see, Father Lurcher is fine.

More gasps and cries, Father Lurcher had got to his feet.

'I am sure he will confirm for us what just took place. The miracle of which I speak.

Shall I tell them Father Lurcher?'

'Oh OK, yes, pp please (?)'

'OK indeed. The incredible act, the miracle we have just witnessed was Glossolalia. The ability to speak in tongues. Father Lurcher here has the gift. He has the gift to imbue the holy spirit, to be consumed by the spirit of God. We must celebrate immediately.'

Raucous cheers and noise. Just when they thought they had it all, this colony of Ludlows found out they were more blessed then any of them had previously thought. What a place this is, they muttered, what a place.

Father Lurcher soon felt the energy return to his body. He was able to celebrate with the rest of the colony. Everything had clicked. The gift of tongues, of course. I knew it. Me and the Holy Spirit eh? I knew it. I am amazing. I truly am.

ah mrs beagle. we're with you all the way mrs beagle. with you all the way

The crazed man had fainted, what was she supposed to do?

Mrs Beagle is a very calm lady. It was this calmness that led her to Father Lurcher that day. The other Ludlows were useless, all panic and hysteria. Mrs Beagle got to her kness and lifted Father Lurcher up onto her lap. She called for a damp cloth and some space for him to breathe. It took ten minutes. During that time she said nothing. She felt concern for Father Lurcher, the whole colony did after that sermon, but she was perfectly calm. It didn't seem too serious to Mrs Beagle. It seemed like the whole colony was exaggerating. A man faints and immediately there is talk of miracles. It was her opinion that Father Lurcher had suffered some sort of heat stroke or overwhelming emotional fit. It was plausible and offered some kind of explanation for the untranslatably slurred sermon and subsequent collapse.

So it came as a shock when Father Lurcher came to, stumbled to his feet, and was declared to carry in his possession the gift of tongues.

In her mind Mrs Beagle had considerable doubts as to the reasoning behind this fast-tracked logic. Being built of tranquil stuff though, she said nothing to suggest there could be a more sensible alternative to the Mayor's shock interpretation. She even, at one point, agreed with a colony member who said that this gift bestowed on them really was astounding and left you feeling totally 'astounded'.

Father Lurcher is not a very calm man. After a few hours partying hard in celebration of his gift, it was pointed out to him by Mayor Harrier, on the way to his new home by the church, that he would require an assistant. It had been a dying wish of the previous Pastoral who suggested, on his death bed, that had he had some full-time assistance perhaps his reign would not have been curtailed so swiftly. To his mind it would almost certainly have prolonged his life by a number of years.

The Mayor's first reaction to the dying man was that a Pastoral does not reign, a Pastoral 'presides' but nevertheless, this was a decent suggestion and would be implemented next time around and as such he could now look on the bright side because this switch in New Luddle policy would ensure his legacy, as the last solo Pastoral, would live on, even if he himself obviously could not.

Father Lurcher gave no pause for thought. That Lady. The one who brought me back, when all thought I was dead. That is she. She will be my... assistant. Like me she is blessed. I feel it. We will do great work together. I am sure.

When Mayor Harrier first informed Mrs Beagle of her new role in the colony she protested. But not for long. Within two weeks she had moved her stuff into the residency by the church where she would sleep and clean and cook for Father Lurcher. As she soon discovered, while she was cleaning and cooking and sweeping and yawning and aching... Father Lurcher likes to spend a lot of his time observing himself in the mirror, singing improvised lyrics like 'Blessed By God (bah bah) He Is Me (bah bah)'. Or asking Mrs Beagle strange rhetorical questions, like: 'You do realize very few people know what it feels like to be a real winner? I mean in the very real sense. But I do. I mean you do realize this don't you Mrs Beagle? You do realize that I feel it every second of the day?' And then skipping off, singing something ridiculous and made up like: 'If I was any one of you – you would be ten times better – hoo hah – yeah bet-tah – yeah.'

So life for Mrs Beagle is tough. She is at the beck and call of this moving body of self-love. And he becks alright, and he calls. He calls and calls.

And Mrs Beagle listens to him. She is nice to him. Obsequious. Attentive. Dutiful. Tired. Lonely. Achy. Non-believing. She does her job. Like she was asked. Like she was told. Full of secrets. No one to tell. Too tired. Too lonely. Too many secrets. No one to tell.

saturday morning with mrs beagle, father lurcher and the new luddle congregation

PART ONE: Saturday service

Mrs Beagle cleans. The service will begin shortly. Father Lurcher is in the church, pumping himself up. Mrs Beagle is in the outhouse where her own service, her tea service, is held after mass. Saturday is Mrs Beagle's favourite day. It is the day that she gets to provide for the community, perform her duty to them rather than to Father Lurcher. It is her honour to provide refreshments to all of New Luddle on Saturday mornings. She takes it seriously. She has pride. She is organised. She has a routine. On the previous night, the Friday, she sets everything up. She brings big metal kettles and fifty cups and saucers and places them on tables laid out especially so as to be accessible but not cause any inconvenience. Each table has a white cotton cloth placed carefully on its surface, some straight, some angular.

Preparation is important. This way she has little to do on the morning itself. All the work is practically done. She is set up. Just needs to light the stove and pour the drinks. Oh, and clean, which is what she is doing now.

Everything must be perfect. Not for him, but for the community. For everyone else. Yesterday, she was cleaning, this time under instruction, and three teenagers came tearing past, they were going to be late for school. It brought a smile to Mrs Beagle's face. She remembered how although she was never late for school herself, she was always secretly jealous of those who were. Maybe it was their courage, or that they just didn't seem to care very much. She wished one day it could be her, at the front of the class, hands on head. It was meant to be shameful, but she had found it heroic. Sometimes she'd slow down her walk. Determined to take the risk, she'd pretend her feet were glued to the floor, scraping them forward in the dust, not leaving footprints but two straight, thickly defined lines. She'd do this for a while, committed, looking forward to the punishment, imagining the thrill, the rush it would bring. Then always she'd look at her watch, see how if she carried on like this she really would be late and eventually anxiety would take over. So often she'd arrive at the school gates, dripping with sweat, searching for breath having sprinted the last way. Never late. In the end she was never late. Not even on her last day at school when she'd made her mind up. So sure she could do it. On her last day she'd been sick and in bed. Annoying, she so wanted to be late for that one time, but, as she always thinks to herself, would she have really gone through with it had she not been ill? Probably not, is what she always thinks. Probably not.

She thinks about these sorts of things a lot.

These memories. They're about me, they're all about who I am. Identity. A summation of myself. If anyone asks what I was like as a child, that's what I'll say. I'll say, remember the one who was never late for school? That's me. I'm the one who never put their hands on their heads at the front of the class. I'm the one who was never late for school. I could be speaking to anyone, anywhere, even Dupont, and straight away they'd know exactly the type of person I am.

Finally, Mrs Beagle has polished the last of the cups. She steps back for a final check, to see that everything is in its correct place. It is. All the cups and kettles, filled and polished, ready and raring. She can go back to the church and take her seat knowing everything is in place for a splendid tea morning. She just needs to sit through a sermon of tongue-speaking first. She rolls her eyes and looks at her watch. It is nearly eleven. She rushes to the door. Opening it wide, she rushes straight into Ferry Doberman.

'Hello Mrs Beagle.'

Clawing back composure and straightening herself out, Mrs Beagle stands upright and takes a pace back.

'Hello Ferry, what are you doing here?'

'I need to speak with Messiah Lurcher Mrs Beagle.'

'Who? Please don't call him that Ferry, his name is Father Lurcher.'

'But He said...'

'Well He probably wasn't being literal. Anyway, it's nearly eleven, the service is about to begin.'

'I know but I really need to speak with him, I thought I could catch him, just before the service. It really is very urgent Mrs Beagle (few drips of sweat, little shakes) I've got to speak with him. I'm worried.

'About what?'

'I can't say Mrs Beagle.'

'Why not?'

'I just can't it's... sensitive.'

'Look Ferry, why don't you talk to me instead, you're too late to speak with Father Lurcher now anyway.'

'Thanks Mrs Beagle but I can't, it's got to be with our spiritual counsellor, I can't see who else I could go to with this.'

'Go to with what? What's this all about Ferry?'

'I've got to go. I'll see him after, it'll be fine, thanks Mrs Beagle.'

Ferry turns and rushes out the door rubbing the back of his head and neck. Mrs Beagle stands, a little confused. Ferry is normally very calm and quiet, focused on his running and that's about it, but just then he seemed genuinely upset. People in New Luddle are never genuinely upset. It must be something to do with his running. She wishes she could have been more help. She wishes Father Lurcher weren't the spiritual counsellor.

Just about every resident of the colony of New Luddle has huddled into the St Bernard church for Pentecostal Pantheists, formerly the St Bernard Pantheist church, until the latest incumbent discovered his gift for tongues, of course. A large crucifix of fruit hangs from a wooden beam above the altar. As the fruit goes black and rots, bits fall down, often splatting Father Lurcher at inopportune moments, like when in the throes of self-love and spirit-conjuring concentration. The funniest time was when Father Lurcher, so focused on his sermon – he's now trained himself to mentally eradicate the external world – that a large chunk of banana fell onto his head, rooted and upright like a yellow horn, he didn't notice a thing. It was still there during the tea morning an hour later.

Since the church was built, Saturday morning service has always been fully attended by the New Ludlows. It is their chance to reflect and be thankful for this society they have developed and nurtured into a sustainable, and more importantly – fair community. On Saturday mornings there is a nice atmosphere in New Luddle. The older ones think about God and all the lovely produce and sunshine that surrounds them. Those of a middling age, like Jennifer Saluki, they think about their children and are thankful and feel lucky that they are able to bring them up in such a peaceful, perfect place like New Luddle. And the younger ones, well they don't think about anything like that. They have been told many times how wonderful their community is, how lucky they are, how important it is for them to continue the good work started by their ancestors, and in truth, the younger ones don't doubt this. Which isn't to say they are free of doubt completely. They doubt there is a God that exists everywhere, lurking in the bushes, staring down from the sun. They doubt Father Lurcher is speaking in tongues. They doubt Victor Poodle is anything more than a figure from history. But this is fine. They don't doubt this a unique and successful society that runs to perfection. They wouldn't change anything. They are happy. Make no mistake, any differences they have in their regard for the community is amiable. It is respectful. Their different voices and opinions don't need to be raised. There isn't a problem. On the contrary, everything is great.

Right on time, Father Lurcher begins the service. Mrs Beagle has reached her seat in the front row with just seconds to spare (never late, remember?). Father Lurcher is silent to begin with. He looks out onto the congregation. They are all there. He's just building tension.

Ferry Doberman is at the back, chewing his nails and sweating profusely, still rubbing his lower neck and back. He's stood with his family, Vera and Donny Doberman.

Beside them at the rear is Bill Spitz. Most of the congregation concentrate on Father Lurcher, give him their fullest attention, but some have already drifted to another world.

Tala Pekepoo is sat on the third row trying to catch the eye of her friend Mardella Shitzoo. They normally like to meet beforehand and sit together but Mardella's mum and dad thought it would be nice if *they* could all sit together for once. Mardella didn't see what was so nice about it, it's not like they were going to have an in-depth chat or anything, it was only sitting in silence. Still, no big deal, she'd see Tala later at the tea morning.

On the second row Gus Brindle and Gerald Pinscher are looking to the crucifix made of fruit hanging perfectly above Father Lurcher's head. They are trying to predict which piece might fall off next. Ten points if their chosen piece makes any sort of contact with Father Lurcher, five bonus points if it's the face or hair. One hundred points if anything sticks to his body or clothing for more than a minute. The score so far this year is – Gus forty-five, Gerald thirty. It's all to play for. Could change in an instant. Both agree, with the crucifix where it is and the amount of older fruit still hanging, today could be a really high-scoring game.

Beth Pointer sits in the front row next to Marjorie and Ken Setter. She sits in the front row so that everyone else is behind her. She makes sure she is one of the first to arrive and the last to get up and leave.

Ned Corgi just stands at the back.

Beth has nothing to worry about, he is the last to arrive and the first to go. He doesn't ever bother with the tea morning. Says he has too many things to prepare for the evening, what with Saturday night being one of his busiest and all. Lots of people think Ned's lost his faith. Since Beth, they think he's stopped being a believer.

The possibly one day, just waiting in the wings, ever ready, you name it we'll be there, NLPD are in attendance of course. The familiar routine. Arriving together, Lieutenant Brett Dachshund elaborately stakes out the congregation before gesturing in their own hand-signing way, to his sidekick Bobby Hound. Bobby invariably looks confused and disorientated, yet to figure out quite what all the hand signing means, and so eventually Brett loudly tells him to take the right side of the church while he takes the left. In these positions they will stand for the duration. It has been noted in fact that Lieutenant Brett Dachshund will often attempt to observe the entire service without blinking. Presumably this is in case he misses any crimes committed in church, in front of the whole colony, in the one millisecond window of opportunity that a blink offers. This is why his eyes water a lot and he looks in pain for most of the sermon. Although Father Lurcher's sermons can sometimes have that effect anyway.

Interestingly, halfway along the second row, Mistress Feist is seated alongside her colleague, the omniglamorous Kelly

Chihuahua. They look so different, so contrasting, a perfect example of how cruel the ageing process can be. The Mistress, all scraped back, dried up, afraid to smile, and Kelly, fresh and flowing, soft and new. Their ages are probably not that different. But they may as well be.

And the Mayor. Bowler hat on head. Looking proud on the front row. Chest out. Good clean chequered clothes. Rarely will anyone sit too close to him. He likes this separation. He thinks it only right. No point pretending he isn't any different. There *should* be space around him. He's in charge of this place after all. Give the man some room.

And on the right-hand side of the fourth row you'll see them. Two boys and a girl. She has long black hair falling in front of her face but it's not quite as dramatic as it has been. One boy looks tired and sickly, the other thoughtful but quiet. Next to them is Jennifer Saluki. She looks happy and is smiling.

Geoff Husky sits alone on the fourth row left. He has a pipe in his pocket, he presses down on the tobacco with his thumb then picks shreds of it out of his browning but yellow nail. This is what he tends to do for most services. Pressing and picking the yellow and brown. Geoff is the only other teacher. His style is withdrawn but comfortable. He is clever. You get the sense, when he talks, that he could probably raise the level of conversation up a couple of notches but he chooses not to. It's because he's nice and doesn't want to come across all 'clever'. And he's used to dealing with children. And Mistress Feist. And Kelly Chihuahua.

Then there's Mr and Mrs Collie. Winston and Geraldine. Second row right. They are two of the oldest residents in the colony. Everybody likes them. Especially Fleece Dingo. He goads them into telling ancestral stories of Old Luddle and the nascent days with Victor Poodle forming the new colony. They know all about previous mayors and use words like 'halcyon' and 'beatitude'. Fleece tells them they should write a book on Luddle history. They could call it 'Ludlow: Old and New – A Brief History' by Winston and Geraldine Collie. Fleece mentions it a lot but feels sad when they say things like, 'we couldn't dear, he wouldn't let us'. Fleece will say: 'The Mayor wouldn't have to know if you were just writing it. It doesn't have to be published or anything, not for years, not till there's a new Mayor.'

'No dear,' they say, 'that won't be possible, you're being silly.'

Now the congregated colony listen. We are about to start.

Mrs Beagle already feels the rumblings of a cringe.

Ferry Doberman still rubbing, still worried.

Tala Pekepoo and Mardella Shitzoo glancing round, looking for one another.

Gus has gone for a bruised apple, Gerald the more ambitious ripened pear.

Beth Pointer, focused in front.

Ned Corgi, distracted at the back.

Brett Dachshund, wide eyed, tears rolling down cheeks, upright, to the left.

Bobby Hound, dreaming of a car chase with himself hanging out the window while driving, shooting freely, he's slumped, to the right.

Mistress Feist, tall back, good posture, if a little stiff.

Kelly Chihuahua, elegant, voluptuous, all health and nature. Looking like she should be sat by a riverbank, dipping her toes.

Mayor Cudrip Harrier, attentive, bowler hatted, stern. Could we also add, if pushed, superior?

The two boys and a girl. One of the boys still looks sickly and tired.

Jennifer Saluki, still happy and smiling.

Geoff Husky, thumb in pipe, shreds under the nail.

Mr and Mrs Collie, second row to the right. Absorbed.

The Lurcher has begun.

An uneven if typically impassioned opening:

'Just look outside. All of you. Go on. Not now of course. But generally. You will see our kingdom, when you look outside. Mine and the Lord's. And what you must remember is that you are free. Free to roam in this kingdom of ineffable beauty. It is in some ways, almost I suppose, your kingdom too. And those that have a kingdom, or those able to freely roam in a kingdom despite it technically not really being theirs, are the blessed. We know that He inhabits the natural world. That is a great knowledge to have. We know that each blade of grass is a hair on his skin. Every sunset a closing of his eye. Only one eye though. The other is of course the Moon. Don't think he sleeps. The thunder you hear isn't him snoring (good one) its... him... c o u g hi, yes, (glee) it's him coughing. He's saying, I'm still here you know, don't for a second think.. . I'm asleep.

'And this is today's message. We holy ones may cough, or blink one eye, but our love never vanishes at night, for we never sleep. For ours is a love that cannot sleep. No matter how tired, or how weary. We never sleep.'

And the sermon is over. Average length. A couple of minutes or so. Five minutes if you include the tension-inducing silence at the start. Now it's time for the finale. Please, brace yourselves. Father Lurcher moves forward, he wants to be closer to the congregation. Silence. With a performer's timing he makes a humble announcement.

'I shall now conjure the spirit of God and speak in tongues.'

There is the sound of people shifting in seats. The faint murmur of giggles. A collective shush of anticipation.

'Where are you Lord? I feel you are close.'

'Ahhhh You are inside.'

'Weeefanula, mustandaham is weeefanula mustandaham. Oh de Oh ma mooo sa saman kinkanteeho'

Father Lurcher's body is now in a strange contortion due to the slight jerking leap he makes as each word comes out, hands floppy and jangling. He seems to have stopped. Run dry. The Spirit maybe doesn't feel like talking. Suddenly Father Lurcher straightens out and stands upright. The biggest grin. He's back. This time Father Lurcher calmly mouths the words. Sadly, the widemouthed exaggeration only has the effect of making it looked badly dubbed, but the performance is so good nobody sees this at all.

'Funtoomala mala ju jen ji jas. Mun fookarita nidly ju je boo ju.

'Muntanada jity kop ko haji kitty ko ko zep zo zon, mistme mo tun shen al tu beet duq me tunani su bree tali can can shu she shep saw ween ty mooow.'

And it's over. Father Lurcher quickly moves down from the altar, out into a typically amazed congregation and begins the clapping of hands – his own applause.

This is his high. A miracle performed. The adulation, the astonishing accomplishment, oh yeah, he believes alright. He is special.

'Thank you, thank you (over-the-top wiping of brow), thanks guys, thank you kindly (arm outstretched, pointing to every person in church), next week yeah, seeya there.'

Ahhh Father Lurcher. He's so cool. A skip, a hop, a swivel, a crash and he's gone. All the congregation can do is catch their breath and make a move for the outhouse. There is a tea morning to attend.

PART TWO: Tea morning

The morning so far has been warm but fresh. Now the heat begins to travel. It comes up through the floor and out of the wooden panels in the out house. It is going to be another very hot day in New Luddle.

Mrs Beagle rushes to get there first. She likes to greet the residents as they enter. A nice hot cup outstretched from her right hand, no one should be waiting around, service with a smile. Slowly, they all start to pour in and the usual good-natured citizens, like Ken and Marjorie Setter, give Mrs Beagle a hand serving the tea. Even the Mayor offers to help, grabbing cups from the side tables, spilling tea everywhere. What's he up to, thinks Mrs Beagle, he's never done that before. But the Mayor is keen: he's whizzing round from one person to the next, fresh cups, refills, empties – you name it, he's onto it. And maybe it's this speedy service, but within a few minutes everyone seems happy, they have their tea and in the warm outhouse the sound is muffled with laughter and tea drinking. Another success for Mrs Beagle.

Sun, Fleece and Daisy stand at the back of the outhouse, slightly away from everyone else. They have brought a big pot of tea over with them. There is much to discuss. Sun has already told them all about last night and Ned Corgi and the liquor and the boxes in the kitchen and sickness on the stairs. Daisy and Fleece are shocked.

'How? How did he get hold of any liquor?'

'Hey, maybe he makes it.'

'How would he know how to make liquor?'

'I don't know Fleece, it was just a guess, you know?'

'He's messed up.'

'That's obvious.'

'Really messed up.'

'What do you think, is it Beth?'

'Definitely.'

'Sad.'

'Very sad.'

'He shouldn't have got you involved though.'

'No.'

(pause)

'What was it like?'

'What?'

'Being all liquored. What was it like?'

'I don't know, sickly, I just felt sick.'

'You gonna tell anyone?'

'No.'

'I don't think you should.'
'I won't.'
'Good.'
'Ned'll work it out.'
'Yeah.'
'(unconvinced) Yeah.'
'Ned'll work it out.'

****

At the other side of the room is Jennifer Saluki. She is enjoying a cup with Ken and Marjorie Setter. Ken and Marjorie are real activists within the community. They are both retired now and love to help out where they can. Mostly they just help Mrs Beagle serve the tea but if there were other things to do you can bet they'd be the ones doing them. The subject has moved to Sun and his imminent employment in the fields. Ken and Marjorie never had children. They are always asking Jennifer about Sun. Nobody knows why they never had children. They seem to really like children.

'I remember my first day in the fields.'

'Here we go Jennifer, you might want to get a fresh cup – this could take a while.'

'Sshh Marjorie, go on Ken, tell us all about it. I'm interested, really.'

'Thank you Jennifer (quick glance and a wink to Marjorie). Best day of my life it was. Fifteen years of living in privilege, having everything provided for me by the citizens, now I could repay them all. I could not wait. I worked it so hard that first day my back hurt for a week afterwards. But it was worth it. I loved every day in those fields, providing for the likes of your Sun, and now it will be his turn to provide for me. It must make you proud, don't it?'

'Absolutely it does, I just wish Sun had your enthusiasm.'

'What, he's not looking forward to the fields? What's wrong with the boy?'

'I know, I know. It's ridiculous. He's OK, he just doesn't seem very excited by it all. Hates talking about it. Says it's a bit early for that talk.'

'But Jennifer dear, he'll be out there in what, six, seven weeks.'

'I know Marjorie, I know. Listen, he'll be fine he's just sensitive that's all.'

'Well, he's been through a lot. If you want me to have a chat, you know man to man, like his father would have done... I mean, sorry Jennifer, I'm not saying..'

'It's OK Ken, that's sweet, but we'll be alright. Don't worry, we'll be fine.'

****

Fleece has gone to talk to Winston and Geraldine Collie about local history. Sun and Daisy stand drinking copious amounts of tea, smiling, occasionally touching hands. Things are different for these two now. They speak about telling Fleece about 'them' and what it will be like, being together. Daisy is happy now and relaxed. The anger is dissipating. When Fleece comes back to inform them of yet another inane story from the New Luddle annals, Daisy goes to get some more tea, leaving Sun to break the news. To say that things between them all are going to be a bit different now. After Daisy walks away, she quickly looks back with a smile, hair pinned behind her ears, she is surely different now. She is happy. He'll make sure she doesn't suffer. Sun watches as Daisy stands by the tea table. He watches as Mayor Harrier follows her to the tea table. As he stands next to her. Sun watches as her face drops.

****

Right near the entrance, stood on a stool, looking out onto New Luddle's dusty paths is Beth Pointer. As usual Beth is sad. As people come over to talk with her, she cheers up and to those in conversation with her she seems fine, her old self, but as soon as they leave, once you see her on her own, you see that really she couldn't be sadder.

****

In his kitchen, Ned is preparing the evening meals. He's thinking about last night. Thinking about how stupid it was to put liquor in Sun Saluki's food like that. He's gotta stop with that stuff. I've got to start thinking for myself. I need to think about what I'm doing.

He swallows what's left in the glass and pours another, then slams his wooden hand hard against the counter.

****

Outside the outhouse Ferry Doberman is pacing around the front steps rubbing hard at his back and lower neck. He's still waiting for his chat with Father Lurcher. He feels it safer they talk alone, away from everyone else, so he is waiting for Father Lurcher to leave. Ferry has red marks at the back of his neck from where he's been picking and scratching. His hair is damp from the sweat. Ferry wishes none of this had ever happened. He wishes he was in running shorts now, that he could just go, at any moment, any time, just go – and if he wanted, never stop.

****

Mrs Beagle is floating. Still serving tea. Pleased that everything is going so well. She offers a cup to Lieutenant Dachshund who is marshalling the front quadrant of the outhouse.

'I'd love to ma'am but I'm afraid I can't.'

'Oh dear, why not Brett?'

'Think you know why, Mrs Beagle.'

(pause)

'No.'

'Ahem, not while I'm on duty, ma'am.'

'But...

8 4

(thoughtful pause)
'Oh, I see. Very well Lieutenant.'
She turns and rolls her eyes, all the time smiling.

****

Patrolling the other side of the room is Bobby Hound. He's guzzling away at the tea like nobody's business. He's scarcely looked up to assess his quadrant once. Lieutenant Dachshund makes a note in the little book he keeps in his top pocket at all times. Bobby guzzling tea - while on duty!

****

Jennifer Saluki is still chatting away with Marjorie and Ken Setter. Ken makes a large coughing sound and apologizes to Jennifer. Marjorie sees if she can find him a glass of water.

****

Fleece isn't the slightest bit surprised.
'It was obvious.'
'What was obvious.'
'You and Daisy.'
'Was it?'
'She told me ages ago how much she liked you, as in you know... liked you.'
'Did she?' (incredulous)
'Yeah, like, a year ago or something.'
'So your not surprised?'
'No,'
'Hasn't come as a little bit of a shock?'
'No.'
(long pause)
'Fuckin hell Fleece.'
'What?'

'Well I'm surprised, it came as a bit of a shock to me.'
(with a smile)
'Yeah, I suppose it would do.'

****

Ken has his glass of water now but still doesn't seem able to stop coughing. Marjorie is patting his back, looking a bit embarrassed.

****

Geoff Husky is handling his pipe stood with Kelly Chahuaha and Mistress Feist. Geoff is talking about history lessons at the school and Mistress Feist is repeating herself, saying, 'Yes Geoff, we'll see, we'll see, I'll speak with the Mayor.'

****

Father Lurcher is always one of the first to leave the tea morning. At the moment he is near the door where he has cornered Winston and Geraldine Collie. They haven't said a word, only listened to Father Lurcher who can speak at length about himself without prompt or hesitation.

'Like I say to Mrs Beagle, put a 2-1 beat behind it and you've got a classic, I mean it's not like I even practise my singing either, it just flows...'

Mayor Harrier is still stood with Daisy. Sun keeps looking over. Daisy has pushed her hair so it covers her face like a long black veil. And she does look sad. She looks mournful.

****

'I should see if she's OK.'
'She'll be fine. It'll just be about summer assembly that's all.'
'What's gonna happen about that?'
'Not sure.'
'She won't back down, you know.'
'I know.'

8 6

'I might have a word with him, the Mayor I mean, think I'll have words.'

'You?' (shock)

'Yeah, me. I'll tell him, leave her alone, she's just expressing her opinions you know.'

'You're going to say that to the Mayor. Sun Saluki. You're gonna start giving the Mayor loads of shit, to his face? Just gonna stroll up. You. Sun Saluki.'

'I will. Look, it's not fair, she's got some good points, I actually think she talks a lot of sense.'

Fleece laughs.

'I thought you didn't get her point. I thought you didn't understand. Couldn't see where she was coming from, you said.'

'Yeah, well maybe I do now.'

'God, look at you, one night on the liquor and you've turned into a right rebel.'

They both laugh.

'Too right.'

****

Both Marjorie and Ken are now coughing and wheezing. The water hasn't helped either of them but Jennifer has still gone to fetch some more. Beth Pointer has come over to see if their alright. Ken is bent down on one knee holding his throat.

****

Father Lurcher decides it's time to go. Ken and Marjorie seem to be hogging the limelight right now, there's a crowd started to gather round. He can see Ken's feet shaking as he lays on the floor, coughing and spitting. Next to them Geraldine Collie has started to splutter about also – she's spitting into her tea. I'll leave them all to it, he thinks. What is this nonsense?

Stepping out, the heat is strong. A swirl of dust carries up into Father's Lurcher's face. Once he's wiped his eyes and brushed himself down he can see Ferry Doberman anxiously calling him over. They walk back to the church together. Ferry stumbling and scraping, almost clinging to Father Lurcher who moves forward with big, bouncing, elegant strides. He is in demand once again.

****

Ken and Marjorie Setter lay on the floor. Both have stopped shaking now. A few feet away, in the arms of her husband Winston, Geraldine Collie spasms a final time. Everyone is gathered round. Sun and Fleece ran over as soon as they heard Jennifer cry out. She's still crying out. Lieutenant Dachshund is everywhere, screaming for everyone to calm down, calling for Bobby, asking for his help. No one is really sure. Mrs Beagle steps forward and tells everyone to move away, to push the circle back, to give them some air. Mrs Beagle crouches over the bodies and feels for a pulse. She touches each of their necks, then their wrists. Finally she puts an ear to their hearts as tears slowly roll down her face. Everyone pulls away further but they know it's too late; these bodies won't accept any more air.

Sun looks round for Daisy. She is still with Mayor Harrier by the tea table. She is collapsed and her body shaking. Mayor Harrier stands over her. He is doing nothing, just standing there, tall and serious. By the time Sun reaches her, she has stopped shaking. Long black hair covers her face. Her body is still. Sun parts her hair out to see her face. He says nothing. She has stopped shaking now.

END OF PART ONE

INTERLUDE

It had been a long while since a resident died. More than ten years. The prevailing belief in the colony is one of natural life cycles. In the old Luddle, people died all the time. People would freeze looking for food, catch pneumonia at the breakfast table. They got used to it. Just the natural life cycle in action. And despite New Luddle being different. Despite New Luddle offering a long life, a healthy life, where death is not frequent and rarely expected, a calm, phlegmatic attitude still presides.

The volume of deaths in the Old Luddle led to an eventual abandonment of funerals or ceremonies. Body collectors would arrive in the night, when most were asleep, carry the dead Ludlow from wherever they had died and push them gently into the ocean. There would be no mourning but a plain awareness that someone had died. People were miserable enough as it was.

Victor Poodle knew that death would be far less frequent in New Luddle but still insisted on assigning a body collector who would carry out the duties of removal and disposal just like before. He said he did it because it helps everyone forget. Funerals and memorials tend to stick in the mind, people want to go visit gravestones, remember anniversaries, be sad for all eternity. No, not here. I'll have no mawkish depressives in my New Luddle. We forget about all of that and move on.

A patch of land at the outer reaches of the colony, near the border, was chosen as a burial ground. Burials would be natural, no coffins or chambers, headstones or sentiment. No visitors allowed. Residents were told the decaying bodies would blend into the soil and the souls of good residents permeate the land. Victor Poodle assured them that even in death residents would still be providing for the colony.

****

Todd Coyote has been New Luddle's body collector for twenty-five years. When he arrived at the burial site, his first visit in over ten years, he was amazed to discover some of the bones from previous burials had resurfaced. White limbs seemed to have sprouted from the soil like ghostly flowers. He replanted them below the surface once more. He hurried it a bit and was sure some of the bones hadn't match the correct skeletons but time was fading away; it would be morning soon and someone might see. Such frustration. It was for reasons like this that Todd really began to question why he volunteered to be the body collector in the first place.

But the job was done. That Saturday night, the bodies of Ken and Marjorie Setter, Gus Brindle, Geraldine Collie and a fourteen-year-old girl named Daisy Spaniel were buried by Todd Coyote, New Luddle's current body collector.

Ordinarily, a death in New Luddle will go pretty much unnoticed. An old person will pop off in the night and on hearing the news people will be sad for a moment but soon cheer up because life in New Luddle is so good. The deaths on that Saturday morning were different. It wasn't the typical old person popping off in the night, it was old and young, and there were five of them. Residents weren't sure how to react. They didn't understand why or how any of this had happened. The whole colony became very depressed. By as late as Wednesday, people were still showing signs of grief and dissatisfaction with the situation. It was extraordinary. Mayor Harrier realized the need for intervention and on the Thursday morning called for a halt to all work and a colony gathering around Victor Poodle's statue, to discuss the issues at hand.

Near enough everyone attended (a couple of teenagers weren't there, that was it). The Mayor stood on a plinth and expressed his concerns for the colony. He admitted that the surprise deaths of Ken, Marjorie, Gus, Geraldine and Daisy were a tragedy that could not easily be explained. There were calls from the crowd demanding an explanation, an enquiry of some sort. The Mayor reminded the colony of their long-standing belief in the natural life cycle. Of course, it normally runs at sixty or seventy years for most people, but this is not always the case. The Mayor also reminded them that very few deaths had occurred in recent times, these were the first in ten years. It would seem, he suggested, that 'our luck has run out'.

But how are we to carry on, how can we just forget and pretend like everything's normal? was the reply from the residents.

Because this is New Luddle, said the Mayor. This is what makes us such an exceptional society. We know that what we are doing every day is right, it's the best possible way to live. We have found all the solutions to those historic puzzles over how best to live. And however hard it is, we have to carry on, we cannot sacrifice the good work. You ask, how can we carry on as normal? I tell you, everything *is* as normal. You just carry on, simple as that, same as before.

The Mayor continued in this vein. He spoke about all the positive things they have achieved and how despite the events of that Saturday morning they should still be the happiest people alive. Look around, he said. Remember, you created this, you live here. There is no place better. Let's keep it that way.

The residents were receptive to the Mayor's comments but you wouldn't say they were especially satisfied as they walked away from the statue of Victor Poodle. He hadn't explained, or attempted to explain, exactly what happened that morning. Over the next few days, however, there were was a definite change in the quality of crops growing in New Ludddle. The tomatoes were flourishing in the heat and all the flowers bloomed with vibrant colour; it was some of the most remarkable produce ever to grow in New Luddle. And residents reminded themselves of Victor Poodle's words. How the souls of the dead permeate the land producing even better crops, and so even in death continue to provide and help. Of course they had always known this was the truth but even so, they were amazed to see what was happening around them. People really began to cheer up. Began working their hardest, determined to make the most of the plentiful crops, and it dawned on them once more just how fortunate they were and how proud it made them feel to be a New Luddle resident.

In perhaps two, maybe three weeks, things were back to normal and everybody (just about) was as happy as they had ever been. It had taken a while but once again all the talk between residents was about the beautiful weather, the wonderful crops, the flavoursome tomatoes and how lucky they all were to live in this place called New Luddle. The natural life cycle carried on as usual; it had thrown them some bad luck of late but it was OK, they'd cope. There were things to do, no point letting it get you down, right? Exactly. It didn't take too long at all before everyone was as happy as they had ever been.

PART TWO

friday morning with sun saluki

There is a bridge in New Luddle that stretches out over a busy commuter track. Cars and trucks grumble and shit along its uneven surface but the drivers – the Dupontians – don't ever look up.

They don't ever see the boy who stands on this bridge every morning looking down. He usually looks for slogans. Just recently he's had other things on his mind.

Sun steps down from the bridge and makes his way home. He goes back to school today. He hasn't been for three weeks. He hasn't spoken to anyone. Jennifer has been smoothing things over with the Mayor and Mistress Feist. She has been very worried; she keeps telling them he just needs time. A little time that's all. To get over the shock. And it's true. She was right. She's been there before. Time has passed and he's a lot better now. It's taken him three weeks. Three weeks where he's pretty much just sat, in his room, looking out the window. Looking at New Luddle. Confused that New Luddle looks so normal. No change. Everything like it always was when all the time he... he can't even sit up and breathe properly without tears and anxiety crippling his face and shaping his hands like fists. But things are a bit better now. Things are alright. Today things feel a little more normal. And that's good. Normal's very good.

Leaving treads in the dust Sun walks as the sun rises high above New Luddle, pounding the fields and tracks, bringing goodness and happiness to the residents. Yep, it's another glorious summer day. That's what they'll say.

A bit too hot for those workers in the fields – definitely too hot to be jogging, thinks Sun, as Ferry Doberman races past, crunching his way around the colony for a second time this morning. And just to the other side of Ferry's route, Tala Pekepoo raises a hand to Sun while reaching to open the door to Beth's cafe. 'Enjoy your breakfast,' shouts Sun. Tala smiles. Sun is starting to feel happy again. Maybe that's it, things really are back to normal. He looks forward to seeing Fleece at school. Not speaking to Fleece was hard. But it wasn't the hardest. He thinks about Daisy. That he won't see her at school this morning. He'll see Fleece but he won't see her. He won't see her anywhere again.

Sun's been thinking but still hasn't worked out how he will cope with the indisputable fact of never seeing Daisy. He isn't sure it's possible to cope. But it must be. You have to get on. He realizes this. Presumably it just happens, over time, without you really doing or thinking that much. Like for his mum. Presumably.

Sun reaches the house. He wipes a bit of moisture from his brow and bangs his shoes against the door frame so as not to bring dust and bits of stone into the house. It's getting hot real fast now, he thinks. Not even the early mornings are cool anymore. The white wooden door frame makes a crashing sound as it whips back into place as he walks in. There is a suitcase in the porch. It has wheels at its base and zips all around. He's never seen one like it. Sun goes on through to the kitchen. Jennifer is there, jumping up and down, smiling, crying, squealing. She's holding someone. She's squeezing tightly. They are both attached and spinning round in circles, the scene is joyous.

Sun raps a couple of times on the door because it seems like the only appropriate thing to do despite it being his own kitchen and one he can usually enter unannounced.

'Mum, what's going on?'

Jennifer releases her arms and de-grips. She turns to Sun. She smiles. The girl she has been holding (crushing) also turns to Sun and smiles. The girl is about 18, Sun thinks, with big eyes and long shiny hair that fluctuates in colour, different shades of blonde reaching all the way down her back. It is extraordinary. They both stand, smiling. Sun is thrown. Unsure, he smiles back and looks to Jennifer with a polite but confused face that says: 'What's going on? Who is this person I've never seen before in my life? Will you please say something?'

'It's Deborah, Sun... she's come home.'

Deborah reaches out a hand.

'Hi Sun, nice to meet you.'

about the jackal family who were best friends with the saluki family until the jackal family had to leave

Sixteen years ago, New Luddle was exactly the same as it is today. While everyone got on with each other - chatting at work, laughing and drinking outside Beth's, generally basking in the dusty happiness that encapsulated the colony from top to bottom – the Salukis and the Jackals were particularly close. Far closer than your average Ludlow. The bestest of friends they were. Maggie and Tilson Jackal, Jennifer and Bryce Saluki.

Quite often, during the summer, work in the fields can be tough and most workers will pair up, to grow, pick and carry the tomatoes together as a team, sharing the workload, therefore reducing the stress and pressure on any one individual. Historically, the scheme, introduced as part of New Luddle's push for labour performance efficiency, has always been a success.

It would have been about twenty-five years ago that Bryce Saluki and Tilson Jackal paired up, a decision that led both of them into the welcoming channels of friendship. It was a friendship that would live with them forever.

Of course, Bryce and Tilson knew each other from growing up in the colony together. They had spoken at Saturday morning tea services and in Beth's cafe. But it was working the fields together that really marked out that rare difference between a mild New Luddle friendliness and the self-imposed, willed familiarity that friends have.

Both men were of a similar age and had been working in the fields for about twelve years. They were good hard workers who, just like all the others, came and left the fields with sweat on their backs and a smile on their faces. But it was within the first few days of working together (sweating and smiling) that Bryce put down his tools and turned to Tilson with an earnest look on his face.

'Can I ask you a question Tilson?'

Tilson moved in closer, stabbing his spade in the ground and resting on the handle.

'Course, what is it Bryce?'

'You like it, working in the fields?'

Tilson thought carefully; it was a very strange question.

'Sure, yeah... I mean of course, it's all part of... New Luddle and that, giving something back, playing a part, making a contribution, you know that.'

'Yeah, yeah I know that.'

Bryce smiled, smiled because it was the answer he expected.

'Why d'you ask?'

Bryce arched his head and looked out beyond the fields, taking in the whole colony with a few deep breaths so it seemed. He wiped his eye from the little particles of dust that forever live in the New Luddle air.

'Not sure really, it's just, *(long pause, to consider)* I mean I understand why we're here, I understand why we do it and why it's good and right and everything and I think it's amazing, you know, what we have here is amazing and I love contributing, I do, I love being part of this community, being a Ludlow, it's just, *(hesitant)* I've been doing it for like twelve years now and I'm not sure... *(thinks)* not sure it's really right for me, you know just on a very individual level.'

Tilson readjusted himself on his spade for a third time but wasn't convincing anyone that he was in any sort of comfort.

'What does that mean, not right for you?'

'Oh I don't know *(slight laugh)* I guess I don't feel that for myself I'm doing anything that great, I'm not fulfilling any

101

personal need inside of me, I'm not living the kind of life that could be lived by me and only me, do you know what I mean? Anyone could be me right now, in fact everyone is me right now and that can't be right can it? I think there must be a requirement in everyday life for the protection of a sense of... uniqueness I guess, that's what I don't feel out here in the fields. I don't feel unique. Bryce Saluki means nothing, has no meaning at all. Just a name. No different to any other. I'm a Ludlow and nothing else. That is my sole identity and... oh I'm sorry it's stupid, I'm ranting like an idiot. I don't mean to... I'm not complaining, honestly, I wouldn't... I don't know how I'd change anything or if I really want to, it's just... stupid. Stupid that's all.'

Bryce became embarrassed. What was he doing talking like that? He didn't dare look up.

And after a while of sitting on his spade, contemplating, Tilson eventually stood up and pulled his spade out of the ground.

'I don't think that's stupid at all.'

For the next few weeks, Bryce Saluki and Tilson Jackal continued to talk. They would find a far corner in one of the fields that was a little more shaded. No one else really worked in the shaded parts as the crops weren't so good. There, they would be out of view. They couldn't be disturbed or overheard. They could sit on their spades and talk, in awkward discomfort they could talk, and talk about anything that ever popped into their heads no matter how strange or unaccepted.

It soon became apparent that neither one really cared about the tomatoes or the fields. They didn't think it was wrong, far from it, they marvelled with all the other residents at how successful and happy a place New Luddle was. They felt terrible about this – but it just seemed that sitting and talking about these things, things that none of the others would ever talk about – imagining other lives for themselves, trading opinion on how the best way to live really was, conjuring imagery of rebellion and alteration, it was fun. It was fascinating. It was far better than growing tomatoes.

Jennifer and Maggie took great delight in Bryce and Tilson getting on so well, as the two women had been friendly for a number of years. Now they had the opportunity to see each other regularly. Most evenings were spent at either the Saluki residence or the Jackals' depending on whose turn it was to cook. A meal and then tea on the veranda. The evenings were fabulous. With hanging flowers scenting the air, the four of them would talk for hours, not like Bryce and Tilson's field talk, there was no controversy in their chatter, but a light banter between friends. They had found a connection and it made them all very happy.

Some years passed and Maggie Tilson became pregnant. It was very exciting news. For the last six months of her pregnancy the baby was all any of them would talk about. What were they going to call it, how great to bring a child into a society like New Luddle, would it be painful, hopefully not, what matter if it was, and so and so on. They promised to all be there, at the birth – Tilson, Jennifer and Bryce, giving their support, clutching hands, shouting encouragement. They promised to look out for this baby did Tilson, Jennifer and Bryce. They promised together. They promised they'd do everything.

The baby was born. About 18 years ago. Deborah Jackal was born. It was a great and exciting time for the Jackals and Salukis. The baby was cared for by all four of them. It changed the direction of conversation for Bryce and Tilson when they were out in the fields; now they talked about rights and responsibilities of bringing up a child, the importance of security and community. The need to grow up strong. They agreed that their children should be allowed to grow into individuals, into themselves, their true selves. Not be forced to go through life, making decisions and believing in things based on schooling and assumption. They will work out life for themselves. They would do what they had to do. What was them, really them. Regardless of expectation. Bryce and Tilson would laugh at this though, because all the while they were saying these things, these obvious criticisms of New Luddle, the truth was, they couldn't think of a safer, happier, better environment to bring up children. They knew deep down this was the best place to be.

And on Deborah's second birthday the Salukis broke the news to the Jackals that Jennifer was now pregnant. The Jackals were delighted but they couldn't disguise their worry. The worry of all four of them.

Deborah had become very ill.

There have never been any doctors in New Luddle. You shouldn't interfere - the natural life cycle and all that, remember? So there could be no diagnosis or real support for the Jackals. Deborah had been losing weight and was fitting almost every other day. Her throat was swelling. She had only just begun to speak before she had to stop. The pain was too much. Certain residents showed more concern than others. Ken and Marjorie Setter were regular visitors to Deborah's bedside. The Mayor popped his head round on occasion. But there was nothing to be done. It was clear to everyone that saw Deborah lying on her side in bed - she was dying. But there was nothing to be done.

Tilson and Bryce spoke. They both agreed that yes, Deborah was more than likely dying, but also it was likely she could probably be treated somewhere. It seemed possible to both of them that somewhere, someone would know of a treatment for Deborah. Somebody could save her life. There must be technology, research, skilled people who do this all the time. We can't just let her die. Tilson was in tears. We must take her to Dupont. There will be someone in Dupont.

Nobody had ever left the colony before. Not as far as anyone could remember. They were an autonomous, self sufficient colony with beliefs and values. They had no need for anyone else. This was how Victor Poodle wanted it. There were to be no relations with Dupont; they would be neighbours in geography alone.

The suggestion that Tilson and Maggie take Deborah over the border to Dupont was extravagant and difficult for people to comprehend. What about the natural life cycle, the equal acceptance of Life and Death? You don't save people, you let them go and then move on. Mayor Harrier heard a proposal. That Maggie and Tilson take Deborah to the doctors in Dupont so that she could get better, and then they would all come back when she was fit and well again.

He took his time, thinking long and hard; he couldn't make a decision on the spot. He would get back to them. A day later Bryce and Jennifer had gone over to Maggie and Tilson's house to hear the verdict. They gathered in the lounge. All of them standing. While Deborah awoke from a sleep, her arms and legs furiously shaking, her second fit that day, downstairs in the lounge the Jackals were told that they may go to Dupont to receive medical treatment – but if they did they would sacrifice their citizenship in New Luddle. On entering Dupont they would become Dupontians and, like any other Dupontian, would not be allowed, by law, to enter onto New Luddle land. They may go, but they may not return. The Mayor could not be persuaded to change his mind. It was final. There could be no return.

****

The thing to remember is, Bryce and Tilson had become the best of friends. Those chats as they sat under leafy trees laughing, imagining countless other possibilities, they had become Bryce's life blood. It's what made him happy. And now Tilson had gone. He tried to reason with Jennifer. He said that moving to Dupont, having their baby grow up in Dupont, a free society, would be the best thing, they could be with the Jackals again, it would be the best thing. But Jennifer was never going to leave. New Luddle was the best place to be. The only place to be. She didn't understand what he was talking about. She only knew that he had lost his best friend. And that he cried a lot. And she knew that he was so sad it was driving him mad. The sadness was driving him and the sadness could lead him anywhere.

'So I was born after you left?'

'I guess so, yeah.'

Jennifer brings over some more tea.

'You can't tell anyone Deborah's here Sun. I mean that. No one. And you'd better go or you'll be late for school.'

'What about this tea?'

'Deborah can have the tea.'

'Thanks Mrs Saluki.'

'Call me Jennifer, please.'

'OK, OK, I'm going, but Deborah, I've gotta ask, why are you here? I mean why have you come back?'

Jennifer has moved over to the sink and begun washing up. Sun puts his bag over his shoulder, ready to leave. He stands, waiting for the answer so he can leave but Jennifer interrupts. She is suddenly anxious.

'That's enough now Sun. Please go. You can't be late.'

'I know, I just want to hear...'

'Sun I'm not sure...'

'It's OK Mrs Saluki. Really. I was just telling your mom before you came in. I'm back to get some information for a college project. I'm investigating the poisonings from a few weeks ago. It's the talk of Dupont, you know. It's how I'm going to become a famous journalist.'

****

'Hey, how are you?'

Fleece and Sun embrace. They haven't seen each other and now it's nice. Like how it should be.

They walk to school and talk. They have a few tears, neither one really knowing what to say but both seem to have achieved some remote level of acceptance that enables them to function. Maybe the refusal by New Luddle to mourn helps. Maybe that is the best way to deal with the really bad things. To get on. To acknowledge that what happens, no matter how big it appears to be, cannot alter the power of everyday existence. Nothing will ever change that – the everyday is forever. Maybe this helps because soon Fleece and Sun are chatting away, catching up like friends who haven't seen each other should. Sun tells Fleece all about Deborah and the story of the Jackals. Fleece is ecstatic but can't believe that Winston and Geraldine Collie neglected to mention this classic piece of local history despite his pestering for gossip and scandal on regular occasions. You've got to remember, this place is pretty perfect, they would say. Nothing much but a contentedness unknown any place else. Cuh, since when was exile a feature of the perfect society, thought Fleece. How content would you feel after being told to get lost? Wait till I see them tomorrow.

'No, you can't mention this.'

'OK. So what do we do?'

'I don't know.'

'I just don't understand. How can she know about what happened? How is that possible? And she called them poisonings. Why say poisonings, where'd she get all this?'

And it dawns on Fleece just what is being said. And it all seems a bit much. He doesn't want to say anything to Sun, but this Deborah girl, she turns up out of the blue and essentially says everyone was murdered? It all sounds very Dupontian.

'Yeah, what makes her think that?'

'We need to speak with her.'

'Too right we do. But she's in hiding isn't she?'

'Yeah, we'll have to sneak her out.'

'Sneak her out to where?'

'Beth's.'

'Really?'

'Yeah, we can trust Beth, and she's old enough to remember, I want her involved.'

They remain serious but there is a touch of excitement in their voices, a bit of exhilaration. There's a bit of fear too.

'Sun... what if she's right. I mean what if it was a poisoning?'

'I know.'

'What, you believe it? But that can't happen here.'

'I know, but it fucking well has and I tell you what Fleece, I want to know who did it because if I know, if I know... I'll fucking...then, (long pause, red face, some spit) I mean if someone did that Fleece, if someone fucking did that... (breaks off suddenly, with tears forming, gliding out from behind his eyes) she was still shaking Fleece, and then, I had her there, she was there... her hair...'

The brief spasm of anger evaporates from around him. Sun is just sad. It isn't really anger he feels, there's no truth there. He doesn't know if there was a poisoning. He has no idea at all. And Fleece knows this. Fleece knows exactly. It's some sort of a channel for his grief, that's all, he isn't sure, isn't sure of anything.

And then Fleece thinks. How do five people just drop dead, all at once? What if it were true? I mean what if it were a poisoning? An intentional poisoning.

Fleece holds his friend for a moment, gives him time to recover.

'We'll get her into Beth's. Then we can talk.'

'OK, fuck it.'

'Oh and also... I shouldn't really be saying this, I feel bad (embarrassed) but er, Deborah's very... well she's kind of good looking, just to let you know, in case you want to pretend you're all cool or something. Just don't act like a dick.'

Fleece laughs. Sun feels a little stupid for saying Deborah is good looking, it makes him feel awkward.

'Alright, shut up, forget it. Let's go.'

'Ok, but I never act like a dick.'

'You are a dick. You can't help it (laughing now) it's who you are.'

'Because you're so cool and everything aren't you? Wanker.'

(pause)

'Dick.'

They run for a bit so as not to be late. They are laughing the whole time, picking up dust, leaving diamond shaped treads. Mrs Beagle can see them from the church. She's cleaning again. She has a scarf on her head to protect her from the heat. It's hard to imagine anywhere hotter and it's not even nine in the morning yet. Still, everyone seems happy. Everyone is happy.

At school nobody says anything to Sun despite his three week absence. Occasionally, during the New Luddle history lesson - which today has been on the type of ship used to cross over from the Old Luddle to the New and how it rotted soon after shoring (elegantly told by Kelly Chihuahua, any mundane passages easily enlivened by an innocent wink or smile) - Sun will stick his hand up to ask if something could be explained again as he'd missed it first time round.

And anyway, Sun and Fleece spend most of the day thinking about how they are going to sneak Deborah into Beth's and what they'll say and just how this whole thing is going to play out. They are excited, it is exciting, but all the while there is a horrible twinge in the back of their minds. What if it's true? What would that mean?

It would mean everything would have to change. It would mean that New Luddle didn't really exist. Because poisonings and murder don't happen in New Luddle. It would mean the end.

fleece, sun and deborah jackal meet up then go to beth's after a bit of planning by sun and fleece

School finishes. Mistress Feist ends the day with a message for all the pupils whose term and schooling is coming to an end. 'What you will go on to do for this community will allow us to continue here, with our teaching, our surroundings, our beautiful and unique lifestyle. Be proud (*big knee-bending wink*) Be a Ludlow.' This final flourish was unusual for Mistress Feist, she just thought she'd give it a go. She hadn't thought it was the sort of thing she'd ever say. It isn't. It wasn't so convincing, but she's glad she added a bit of oomph at the end.

Sun and Fleece exit and head straight for the dust track to the side of the school. They straddle the gate and are soon engrossed again. A fast pace, they have to squint when looking at each other because the dipping sun keeps interfering, finding their eyes like targets. The dust track is right at the back of the colony near the commuter road. Occasionally they hear the horn from a truck and see a bit of smoke crawl upwards from the road but they pay no attention to this. There's stuff happening on their side of the road today for a change, they don't have time for Dupont right now. No, right now New Luddle is the place to be.

And in New Luddle Sun Saluki and Fleece Dingo are making every effort. They need to think things through, come up with answers. They need some sort of a plan.

'Right. I'll go to Beth's now and explain everything. I'll ask if Deborah can come over so we can all talk in private. Beth'll understand, I can persuade her.'

'Good. I'll just go home then. That's easy. What time shall we meet?'

'It'll have to be after dark so we can sneak Deborah in, and Beth's will be closed so there shouldn't be too many people around.'

'OK, you're sure there's nothing else I can do?'

'No. I'll see you at Beth's at nine o' clock.'

'Yeah, good luck with that.'

'Won't be a problem.'

They split. Fleece goes home to wash and attempt a sprucing up. Sun heads to Beth's where he knows it will be busy with workers finishing the day with some tea and cake. He thinks about what he's going to say but isn't concerned because he knows Beth. He knows she'll be on their side. She'll help. She likes them.

****

Sun only needs to spend a few minutes with Beth. She is shocked and refuses to believe him. She was around Sun's age when the Jackals left. She laughs in disbelief, saying how funny it is, she had completely forgotten. She says that if Sun hadn't said anything she probably would never have thought of the Jackals and how they had to leave because of poor little Deborah, ever again. It was like she'd somehow blanked it out. Isn't that awful, she says. How we do that, just blank things out.

It takes her a few minutes to digest what is being said. She remembers how she would sometimes pass the Jackals' house some evenings, when it was really hot, like now, and they would be sat out on the veranda with Jennifer and Bryce, laughing and joking, pouring drinks for each other. They'd all wave at her and call her name. They were so nice. They always had lots of flowers on the veranda, you could smell them from the back of the house. They talked for hours out there. They were, they were so nice.

Sun sees that Beth is getting upset so he cuts in by asking if it's OK if they come over to hers, somewhere they can talk it through. Beth wholeheartedly agrees. Sun knew it. Beth's great. She really does like us. And she wants to meet Deborah. She's desperate to meet Deborah.

****

Sun knocks on the door of the spare room, where Deborah is unpacking a few clothes. Jennifer can be heard downstairs banging things about in the kitchen. Dinner was strange. While Jennifer is delighted that Deborah's come back - she never thought for a second she would ever see her again - she's also become a bit panicky. She's worried she's doing something wrong by New Luddle and might get in trouble for it. Or, just to be clear, she knows she's doing something wrong by New Luddle that will get her in trouble, and it's making her panicky. That's why she's banging things about in the kitchen. Her head is full of thoughts about Deborah and Maggie and Tilson. It's brought back memories, lots of memories, not very nice memories, lovely beautiful memories, painful memories, the happiest of memories, memories of laughter and sunshine, memories of people leaving, never to come back, friends disappearing over a border. And Bryce. His face.

But she knows that she is doing what she has to do, because most of all she remembers the promise she made. The promise they all made as they stood around Maggie. An exhausted Maggie who is holding a baby, a brand new baby only just born and they surround her and they make their promise. To look after her no matter what. To care for the child in whatever circumstance occurs. To be protectors. Forever.

And she has to do that. For Maggie. For Tilson and for Bryce. She has to look out for this child and take good care of her.

Sun enters the spare room and is immediately caught unawares by the huge smile Deborah greets him with. It forces him to walk straight into the corner of the bed and means he will have to continue in pain without being able to rub or show any signs of anguish.

'Hey, how you doing Sun. Ouch, you alright?'

'Yeah, sorry er listen Deborah, we need to talk. This is going to sound ridiculous but can we sneak out later when it gets dark and go to Beth's cafe? There are some people I want you to meet (*pause, bit confused*) And that's when I'd like to talk. Because we need to talk, so... you know that's when I'd like to do it.'

'OK, yeah, I'd love to sneak out after dark. Sounds exciting.'

Another massive grin.

Cool, says Sun, as he leaves the spare room hoping to bypass all the furniture and let Deborah carry on with her unpacking.

He wonders how long she intends to stay and what will happen while she's here. For some reason he's starting to feel good again.

He's starting to feel more alive because he knows if Daisy were here, she'd be on top of this poisoning thing, she'd be all over it, accusing, demanding; she wanted this place to change. She willed it. Every single day she willed it. Until those last few days with her, Sun had always thought she was crazy to want this, he didn't understand. He thinks he does now. He thinks he gets it exactly. He can't wait to hear what Deborah is going to say. He's right behind Daisy on this one, he's with her entirely, because he knows she's on top of it. She's all over it.

Sun smiles. For the first time he thinks of Daisy and just smiles, no tears, no convulsions or angst. A happy smile. Her hair tied back. Whatever happens she's gonna love this. She's going to be right up for this. And I'm going to be right by her side, thinks Sun. I'm going right there. All the way. Me and her. All the way.

Sun is happy. Everyone is happy. In New Luddle, everyone is happy.

****

Despite moderate protest Sun has made Deborah wear a scarf over her head. It is nearly nine o' clock and completely dark outside. Sun has mapped out a route. They walk behind the houses. Most people are inside or on their verandas. It is unlikely they will pass anyone in the streets at this time. Still, Sun keeps a watchful eye. Sun keeps having to shush Deborah as she giggles.

'This is fun.'

'Nearly there, it's just a bit further along, where that light is.'

'I like this place. It's cute. I bet everyone attends the church on Sundays, don't they? With a bake sale afterwards. It's sweet. Reminds me of parts of Dupont. The weird parts. No offense it's just...'

'Shush. We go to church on Saturdays (whispering) And what the fuck's a bake sale?'

'My God, your language. I don't believe it. Sun it's terrible. I thought you'd be all dams and dash-its and golly gosh. This is great. It's so funny.'

'Deborah, please stop finding everything funny. Nothing here is funny. It's pleasant. It's happy. And to be quite honest Daisy always said it's good to swear because it would make us feel better. Like we actually existed in this place. It offered a bit of danger, makes us different to all the others. She said it was normal, or that it should be normal, honest expression or something like that. At the time I wasn't sure. Now I know what she meant. That's why we swear. We kind of like it. It's not a New Luddle thing alright? It's just us.'

'Sorry about Daisy.'

'So am I.'

(silence)

'Right, here it is.'

1 1 5

They enter Beth's cafe, Sun wincing as the door creaks and slams. Deborah apologises and giggles. Sun tuts and rolls his eyes. Why does she find everything so funny?

'So where are your friends?'

'Upstairs.'

There are no lights on downstairs but the lights upstairs illuminate the staircase so Sun and Deborah can easily find their way. In the sitting room Beth is standing with a cup of tea. Fleece has a piece of tomato cake stuffed in his mouth. His attempts to swallow the cake in what he thinks will be before anyone notices creates quite a scene and Deborah's first words on entering the room are 'is he OK?' Sun pats Fleece on the back and smirks at his friend.

'Yeah I'm fine, just a bit of er.. cake got caught that's all. I'm Fleece by the way. Fleece Dingo.'(shake of hands)

'And I'm Beth. How do you do Deborah, it's been a long time.'

They all sit in Beth's sitting room. Beth is excited to meet Deborah and keeps a constant flow of tea and cake coming. She tells Deborah all about the fuss and scandal when she and her family left. Deborah replies with stories of her early childhood spent in hospitals where she would wait for months on end in a big queue for the operations she needed. She said that sometimes her dad refers to Dupont just like that. He'll say, 'do you know what, I sometimes think that's all this place is - one big queue for the hospital.' But eventually she got better, they found out what was wrong and cured it. So instead of dying she lived and grew healthy and strong and here she is today. Back home.

It's her first year in college and the summer project, where grades count towards what job you get (is what she has been told) has to be a good one. She wants to be a journalist and what better story than the Dupont poisonings. With no Dupontians allowed in to investigate and interview, it's all been speculation so far, just hearsay. So that's why she's come back. She's come back to her home town to break the story. And after she'll be a famous journalist. Famous and rich. Rich and famous. Whatever, she's going to be it.

Sun lifts his head and pushes his chair forward.

'Right then, about these poisonings.'

In the quiet comfort of Beth Pointer's sitting room, on a rug, on a chair, with tea and cake, Deborah Jackal tells them what she knows.

'People in Dupont often speak about New luddle. They call it Fuddle Luddle. They think the people are religious freaks who inter breed and live off seeds. Some say they are a mute community. Others make predictions stating the women of Dupont aren't allowed to leave their homes, that many are blind because they've never seen daylight. For most, actually no, for all Dupontians, New Luddle is a joke. A weird little plot of land inhabited by even weirder people living some strange puritanical life. But besides the silliness nothing is ever really said or written about. Yet, a couple of weeks ago, all the newspapers ran with this story of mass murder in a church hall. Somebody had poisoned the tea after church one morning and five people had died. This quaint little backward community had been devastated by the attack. People were distraught. Nothing like this had ever happened in New Luddle and the events had thrown a dark cloud over the community, which was in deep depression. It was breaking news.'

'But who broke it?' (Sun)

'Good one, yeah who broke it?' (Fleece)

'The press in Dupont refused to disclose the source of any information saying that confidentiality contracts had been signed, but clearly there is a mole in New Luddle. Somebody is feeding information across the border. It's never happened before. Never has Dupont known with any certainty what happens in the colony but now it's receiving first hand accounts of dramatic events. Now

New Luddle isn't quite so funny. There's a human angle, see. People died. Good people. Their friendly neighbours who want nothing but peace and a sustainable life. A tragedy has occurred. But as for who the mole is, the feed, the communicator general - it could be anyone in the colony.'

'It's not possible.'

'You'd better believe it Fleecy. This is real.'

'Actually, Deborah it's just Fleece and I'm telling you it's not possible.'

'Listen. I read the stories. I watched the news. This is happening. People in Dupont are talking about the poisoning. It must be possible because it's happened. People hundreds of miles away will be talking about it right now. So what are we going to do?'

Beth stands to clear some plates. Part of her initially felt like she was indulging these young people, but clearly if Deborah was telling the truth, and there was no reason to think she wasn't, then things were serious.

'But Deborah, what poisoning? You have got it wrong to an extent dear. There was no poisoning. It was a tragic accident.'

Beth looks around at the three of them with a confident smile, a smile suggesting she'd pointed out some obvious and crucial defeating fact and was a bit sorry to spoil all the fun. But the response of Deborah, Fleece and Sun was chilling. Clearly they were all now convinced a poisoning had taken place. They looked back at Beth and she knew what they were thinking.

'What are you saying, someone intentionally set out to kill Marjorie and Ken, Geraldine, Gus? Daisy! You can't be serious (*hysterical laugh*) no, you're taking this way too far. Do I really need to remind you where you are? It's not downtown Dupont that's for sure. I'm sorry Deborah I don't know what the folks from Dupont are saying but they are wrong and so are the three of you. You're all wrong.'

Out of breath, Beth sits back down.

'But the deaths are suspicious. I mean you don't just drop down dead from a cup of tea. It was five people, Beth, all at the same time. I know this doesn't seem like an option to you but when you think about it and I mean really think about it, what other serious option is there?'

'But who would do such a thing?'

'Maybe the same person who's leaking all this information to Dupont.'

''Why? This whole thing makes no sense and I'm not sure I should be having this conversation with you lot. I'm sorry but this is wrong. We shouldn't be talking like this. It's wrong.'

'Beth I understand what you're saying but what if it's true? What if someone killed Daisy? You expect me to sit around and do nothing? Pour some tea, pick some tomatoes, smile and go to church. You think I can do that for the rest of my life knowing someone in this colony killed her?'

'No, of course not Sun. Oh I don't know. It's getting late. Maybe there's something in it, I'm not sure, but the question remains, what can any of us do about it anyway?'

There is a long silence. Deborah has gone a bit quiet; maybe she's starting to understand maybe the seriousness of these implications. Sun rubs his eyes but there is a determination about him now. He's willing to explore himself, he feels freer and more in control. Nothing is quite so predictable. He likes it. Truth and reality were starting to take prominence in his mind, in all of their minds and that was unusual. Ludlows weren't meant to think like this and he begins to realize just how restricted the lives in this colony were. He's ready for a change. Now is the time.

Fleece has been sat in the corner the whole time. He has listened to the various voices and questions as they came and passed through, in and out of his ears, but really he's spent the time thinking to himself, raising questions and answers in his own mind with regard to this very central question of what can be done. Possibilities and potentialities have been swirling about, coagulating nicely so that now he feels confident. Yes, absolutely. That's it. He's got it. Yes, he thinks, that's the fucker. He sits up, places his mug on the tea table with exaggerated assurance, and declares that he has a plan.

'Deborah – you will have your story, you will have your fame and success, and we, Sun – we will have our justice.'

Sun smiles with excitement. Beth finally breaks with a nod of agreement. Deborah looks away, annoyed with Fleece for making her feel like a selfish outsider. Annoyed, and also a little ashamed.

But there is a plan now. There is reason for optimism. Sun, Fleece and Deborah seem to have convinced Beth and Beth agrees that there must be some sort of investigation, the culprit (or culprits, as was discussed well into the night) must be brought to some kind of justice. She realized herself that, like the others, this news and discovery had sparked something inside her, brought her back to life almost. She has spent these last years hiding, ignoring, trying to forget reality. Now she found herself trying to chase it, trying to hunt reality down. That's what they all were now: hunters on the march.

sleep well new luddle, sleep well

Sun sits up. He can't sleep. Too busy thinking. The thoughts are of Daisy. But they are not sad thoughts because he has come to a recent conclusion that she is with him. She inhabits him now. She has come back. And found him. Sun realizes this is what happens after death. It's how it works. You find someone to go inside. You enter through them. You live in them. You sleep in them. It's where you find warmth and comfort and it's the place you'll be forever.

So you have to make the right choice. And this is what's woken Sun, this recent conclusion and what it means.

It's a comforting thought, that they are reunited once more, but also puzzling because when he eventually dies, who then does he go inside? Although it won't just be him, will it? It'll be him and Daisy because she is inside him. Who do they go inside? Wow. It's like those Russian dolls, entering into bigger and bigger bodies, is that what he means? Is that really his depiction of an afterlife? Russian dolls. Because that's rubbish depicting.

He doesn't know. He doesn't want to choose, doesn't want to think about it actually, he's tired. I shouldn't be sorting out where I'm going to live after I die, it's not something I need to think about.

Maybe he's wrong. Maybe this thing with Daisy and him is a one off. That makes him very lucky. Very lucky. He thinks this as he slips off back to sleep. Him and her. Her and him. All the luck.

< >

The red tape is in sight. He takes one look over his left shoulder and another quick glance over the right, just to be sure, because it would seem like there's no one near him, he's way out in front, after that difficult first ten miles he's been gradually pulling further and further away from the pack so that now when he looks behind there is nothing but empty road as far as the eye can see. He can relax, all the training, the preparation, it's really paying off, he can relax for these last few yards.

And the jubilant crowd erupt as the tape is broken, the flashes from cameras a dense and emphatic display of blinding sparkles. He's done it.

He can come home and show the trophy to the Mayor and everyone else in New Luddle proving it was the right decision to allow him to enter. Ahh the vindication. The satisfaction of victory. He's done New Luddle proud and nobody will ever forget.

< >

Jennifer is holding out the baby, 'you want to hold him?'

He's crying. Bryce is crying. 'yes please.'

FLASH

All sat on the veranda. 'I'll fetch some tea.'

'It's another beautiful evening ain't it?'

FLASH

'They're going Jen, they're going. Do you know what this means?'

FLASH

'Bryce, calm down it's OK, look at you, what's wrong?'

FLASH

Jennifer shouting. 'Sun stays here with me, I don't care about your "suggestions".'

FLASH

Bryce shouting. 'What is happening to me? What's going on?'

FLASH

He's holding on to the baby, so carefully. 'It's OK, Sun isn't made from glass.' They laugh. 'I'll protect him like he is though, I'll protect him like he's the most delicate substance in the world.' And Bryce smiles, looking into Sun's eyes, he smiles.

Jennifer stirs, turning on her side.

< >

'You're under arrest motherfucker now get on your knees. Ahhh nice of you to show your face Sergeant Dachshund, sadly you're two minutes too late I had this one figured out from the start. You can buy me a... house (no, ridiculous) ... dinner (not bad but...) ... new hat (perfect) yeah you can buy me a new hat to make up for your shoddy and... really bad police work. And maybe next time you'll be here in time to learn a few things from the Houndster himself - Lieutenant Bobby Hound.'

< >

Fleece closes his eyes once more.

I don't know why I'm thinking about her. She's just some dumb Dupontian who's only here to try and make her life in Dupont better because she'll have money and a big house. She's using us, she couldn't give a shit about New Luddle or Daisy or anyone. She's just out for herself. I wish she'd just go away, go away and get out of my stupid dreams.

< >

'Who, that Kelly Chiauhua? Hardly. That's not how I define beauty Mistress Feist. No that's not real beauty. Now real beauty, erm would you mind? It's just I need to stare deeply into your eyes for this, that's if you want me to go on describing what I would call real beauty, and ahem, exuse me if I get a little lost on the way.'
'Why, kind Sir.'
'No, donít speak.'
'Oh. OK... sorry.'

< >

Suddenly, with a jerk he is awake. He lifts up his hand. Some of the varnish has peeled off. They said it never would but it has. It is stained with tomato. He gets out of bed and goes to

the chest of drawers which has a half filled bottle and an empty glass on top. He takes the bottle and gets back into bed. He doesn't need the glass. He won't sleep again tonight. He'll lay awake and think about her. Think about her all night long. And he'll finish that bottle because it takes away the pain. And the bottle does take away the pain. And it leaves a man who is scarcely alive any more.

< >

Mrs Beagle doesn't have any dreams tonight but a little further down the corridor, in Father Lurcher's room, there's all sorts going on.

'An ascension? For me? Into heaven? But why?'

'God just thinks it best you pop up here for a while, he'd like your help.'

'But I like it here, in New Luddle, this is where I serve.'

'Well, to be frank, God disagrees, he rather fancies you might be better off up here with the angels and so forth.'

'But I can speak in tongues! This is crazy, have you seen their faces? They love me, they're amazed by me.'

'I'm sure they are, but lets be clear, the ascension will be public, I mean it's a trump card really, nothing beats an ascension.'

'Oh come on, er hello - resurrection.

'Oh yeah.'

'No I'm really not sure about this. I'll have to speak with him personally, is he around?'

'Er, yeah I guess, he's kind of everywhere yet nowhere, it can get a bit confusing. No, hang on, there you go, here he is.'

And the colours change, the dream shifts, a more crumpled filter.

In bright light a vision appears, but in Father Lurcher's dream God is not a man but a woman.

'I want you to leave New Luddle, Father.'
'But, please.'
'You're not real and nobody needs you.'
'Please Mrs Beagle, please.'
'No Father, just go.'

Mrs Beagle shrinks as she heads skywards, back to the heavens.

But already a new dream has begun and phew *thinks Father Lurcher, as when Mrs Beagle left to go back to heaven she seems to have left some dancing shoes and a cane behind, and – wait a second, is that music in the background? It is, you know, and Father Lurcher is smiling, a crowd is gathering, the adoration is back, he's in full swing...* Thank God for that.

the police hut, fleece's plan,
the investigation begins...

PART ONE: Bobby and Brett get a surprise

It is very early on Saturday morning but New Luddle's provisional police force and, in particular, head of provisional NLPD, Lieutenant Brett Dachshund, are not of the opinion that potential criminals have any regard for how late or early it is on Saturday mornings. That is why they have been sat in their police hut for some considerable time now playing gin rummy. But really, says Brett Dachshund, they aren't playing gin rummy at all, they're playing the 'waiting game'.

'You sure know your card games Boss.'

'No, Bobby, it's not a card game, I'm just pointing out that when we sit here for days on end, it isn't really wasted time because what we are doing is waiting, biding our time for when the crime starts and we can open that drawer, put on the badge and get to work. That's what we do every day Bobby. Play the waiting game. Apart from your regular training sessions of course, which by the way will be focusing on covert operations and the use of disguise today so it should be a good one.'

'Great. Sorry again about last week.'

'Don't worry about that Bobby, I think I can handle the odd blow to the head, part and parcel Bobby, part and parcel of this job.'

'You were out for a while though Boss.'

'Mmm, it is a bit sore.'

Despite Victor Poodle's instruction that a potential police force be installed as a 'just in case' measure, at no point has it ever been suggested by a resident that something criminal has occurred which would require a police involvement. Indeed, on certain occasions, at meetings and forums, it has been suggested by residents that the very existence of a provisional police is so unnecessary that it should be closed down so the officer and trainee officer could then help in the fields. 'They are of no worth to the community sat in that shed all day with nothing to do but sleep and play pretend,' goes the argument. Pretty hostile stuff for New Luddle. But as is always pointed out, it was Victor Poodle's idea and you don't argue with Victor Poodle. Not ever. So the provisional police have continued throughout the years to sit in the police hut and play the waiting game. Or gin rummy. Or both. It seems to be all the same anyway.

'More tea Boss?'

'Why not Bobby, why not, and I think we should swap quadrants at church this morning. It's good to have something different to look at now and again, plus it confuses the crims and shows we're on our toes.'

'Right Boss, but I do sometimes wish we didn't always have to be on our toes. It would nice if we could be on our bottoms now and again. Father Lurcher can go on a bit and I get dreadful leg ache sometimes.'

'Goodness me Bobby, what are you talking about? When I was a young trainee...'

And then something very strange happens, something that had never happened before. There is a knock on the police hut door.

'Erm, did you hear that Boss?'

'I certainly did Bobby, it's caught me a bit off guard I don't mind telling you. What's your assessment?'

'Not sure. We could see who it is?'

'OK, that's your call Bobby, but just remember if it's some hard case criminals who have come to kidnap and torture us so they can rampage round the colony, well, you'll have to live with yourself, that's all I'm saying Bobby, you'll have to live with yourself.'

Lieutenant Brett Dachshund opens the door to Fleece Dingo, Sun Saluki and Deborah Jackal.

'Lieutenant Dashund may we come in, we have some very serious police business to discuss with you. It is really quite urgent, we just had to come to the authorities straight away.'

'Well that is quite right, you must come in. Please sit down. Sergeant?'

'Yes Boss?'

'Make some tea for these good people.'

And so it goes. Sun, Fleece and Deborah sit down and explain everything.

'I mean you must have thought it suspicious Lieutenant?'

'Erm. Absolutely. I mean, of course. Very suspicious. Very suspicious indeed. I have a nose for these things. Years of training you know. But the Mayor did explain all this, what with natural life cycles and the law of averages, what was it? No deaths in ten years? so in fairness, we were due about five. Isn't that right Bobby?'

'Yes Boss... I think, I mean, really? We were expecting five people to die were we? That is news. To be honest Boss, I don't remember anyone mentioning it to me. But then I can get distracted sometimes.'

'Exactly Lieutenant. Which law of averages says five people, all of different age and health, will collapse and die in the space of a minute? It's ludicrous. That was the Mayor trying to calm everyone down. There can only be one true explanation. They were poisoned. You must agree. You must see what has happened.'

'Now steady on. I mean, do you realize what you're saying here? You're saying murder, in fact you're saying mass murder. There is no more serious crime.'

'We know Lieutenant, that's why we came to you. You're the only one who can do anything about it. The only one who can solve the mystery and bring the criminal to justice. It's your job now. You're activated. You are the power in this colony. You are the Lieutenant. A real Lieutenant. And this is homicide.'

'Hang on, everybody just calm down.'(*tingle of excitement-possibility*)

Lieutenant Brett Dachshund stands with his tea. He is shaking his head and speaking slowly to himself, he's running through everything that has been said, filtering, assessing, getting a handle on the situation.

Five dead. Different ages. All in the space of a minute. All in the same room. Everything at once. What happened. Natural life cycle. Unlikely. Tragic bad luck. Can't be. Poisoning. Murder. Makes sense. Something in the tea. Two of them young, healthy. Wouldn't keel over and die. Impossible. Unless. Poison. Murder.

And then it all clicks. Lieutenant Dachshund stands motionless. He takes a deep breath and holds out his chest. He raises his head.

'Bobby. Go to the drawer and get out those badges. We've got a case to solve. And the criminal just made a big mistake.'

Then an almighty 'yeeeeha!' and Lieutenant Dachshund is bouncing, grabbing Bobby by the shoulders, a more buoyant man there has never been. 'You're ready for this boy, believe me you're ready, this is it, what we been waiting for all our lives. Step aside New Luddle, the police are in town...'

But Bobby doesn't seem quite as enthused as everyone else (even Sun, Deborah and Fleece have been up on their feet giving fives up high).

'What is it Bobby, don't you know what this means?'

'But you're forgetting something Boss.'

'Am I, what? We've got the badges, we don't have to put the hats on now do we?'

'No Boss, it's just, I don't want to be no killjoy or anything but we can't be the NLPD until the Mayor agrees a crime has been committed and he doesn't think there has, does he? So I don't see how this all gonna happen now do you?'

Lieutenant Dachshund sits and wipes his brow, breathes heavily from the excitement, and sinks in his chair. Dejection kicks in instantaneously. The speed from high to low has sent him dizzy and full of nauseous disappointment.

'Goodness me Bobby, you're absolutely right. The Mayor won't admit a crime has taken place and until he does we're powerless. I'm sorry kids. Bobby's right; how's this all gonna happen now?'

A response of smiles and sniggering leaves Brett and Bobby utterly baffled. Exchanging cheerful glances with one another Sun and Fleece look to Deborah who stands to address the confused wannabe crime-busters.

'Fear not Lieutenant Dash. We figured this would happen, that's why Fleecy here has come up with a genius plan.'

Deborah has a whopping smile on her face and is bouncing on tiptoes. Brett Dachshund and Bobby Hound are bewildered (what a morning!) and while Fleece is on the one hand thankful for being acknowledged as inventor of the genius plan he is on the other irritated at persistently being called Fleecy. It's a lengthening of the name for a start. Ridiculous.

'Now, you doubtless know Fleece (*thank you*) and Sun, you see them all the time. But does either of you have any idea who I am?'

'Well yes, of course we do, don't we Bobby?'

'Absolutely Boss, that's an easy one. Although I am struggling a little bit with a name... and the face isn't exactly what you'd call familiar.'

'Erm, yes now you come to mention it. I too seem to have gone blank all of a sudden.'

'That's because I am not from here. I am from Dupont.'

Bobby and Brett both spit out noises that resemble nothing like words. Now they're really confused.

'But you can't. It's not allowed. You can't. Bobby? Can she? She can't.'

'You're right on this one Boss. She can't. It's not allowed.'

Deborah explains. Bobby was just a bit too young to remember but Brett has a vague recollection, although he was a committed trainee at the time and had little interest in the goings-on in the colony. Unless they might be criminal of course. Which they weren't.

'Now. When my parents left, Mayor Harrier made it quite clear that should any of us return to New Luddle it will be as if it were a Dupontian stepping onto New Luddle land. This as you are well aware is a criminal act as set out by Victor Poodle himself during the original negotiations for the creation of the colony New Luddle.

(*dramatic pause*)

'So then Lieutenant Dash, here I am. Arrest me.'

Sun and Fleece stand and clap. It truly is a genius plan. Fleece gushes with pride. Deborah seems ecstatic with her own performance and the show-stealing final demand for her own arrest, arms outstretched in mock handcuff.

But Bobby and Brett are a little slower on the uptake. Bobby just looks a little confused but mostly vacant whereas Brett Dachshund is stood, head down, filtering again.

Leave for Dupont. Told any return will be as a Dupontian. No Dupontians allowed.

Illegal for Dupontians to be here. Deborah is here. In the hut. Born a Ludlow now a Dupontian. She is here. That is illegal. It was Mayor Harrier's decision.

He's the one who said it... he decided... he can't deny... can't deny... the crime...

His face lights up, his mouth wide and smiling, tall again, he speaks.

'Bobby, pass me my badge will you, and get the hats. The NLPD has a criminal to catch.'

PART TWO: The NLPD go about their business like the professionals they are

A few minutes of jubilation, a quick check on the time, just one hour until mass begins, and Sun makes calming gestures. He makes it clear that a murder investigation is a serious thing ('it's as serious as murder itself' - Lt Brett Dachshund) and they need to do some planning, and quick.

Deborah dives straight in.

'OK, we need suspects, we bring them in and we break them down. They don't leave here until we see a signed confession.'

Deborah gives an exaggerated wiping of hands and a down turned mouth to suggest that crime solving is quick and easy as long as you don't mess around.

But Lieutenant Dachshund has his own methods and as he makes clear, he's leading this investigation.

'I thank you, all of you for your help in bringing this to my attention, and in return we will act as a unit to solve this case, but I must stress, this is a small colony and an investigation will be handled with sensitivity and guile. We don't rush in. We work through that fateful day. We spot inconsistencies, unusual behaviour, then we casually start asking a few questions, just subtle, we don't wanna arouse too many suspicions and we see what reaction we get. That's how it's going to work, people. There aren't too many residents in this colony and one of them is a murderer. So we keep to that strategy. OK? Now let's revisit that day.

It's impressive. Obviously he's been training for years but nonetheless he's risen to the challenge with immediate skills of leadership and organization. To be honest, the other four in the hut are struck by his sudden charismatic dominance. Yes, they will do as he says, he's in charge after all.

'OK, let's start thinking about that day. It was a hot morning, Saturday, so church morning, the colony gathered at church, just like always, but think everyone, think, what did you see? Was there anything strange in anyone's behaviour? Was anyone missing?'

They each sit and contemplate and it goes very quiet. Bobby is the most animated. He's scratching his face, rubbing his head, sat up, sat down, he's giving it some serious thought.

'I've drawn a blank Boss. Those church mornings are all the same. It was just like any other.'

There is a dejected nod of agreement from the unit. Already the Lieutenant's confidence is dwindling despite the authoritative start.

Bobby sits down again.

'I mean there was that Ferry Doberman of course. He was all over the place. It was late, just a minute or so before Father Lurcher was due on; came running from the outhouse he did, in a right state... always running isn't he? I wanna say to him, "Slow down Ferry, what's the rush?" I suppose I could now, I mean legally, you know, if I thought he was a... hazard?'

'Goodness me Bobby. Did I hear you correctly? Ferry Doberman came rushing from the murder scene in a distressed state just before mass?'

'That's right Boss.'

Everyone stands up. Deborah is the first to get carried away. 'Let's nail him. We bring him in, apply the pressure, he'll crumble.'

Sun isn't so sure.

'Where's the motive? Why would Ferry poison anyone? I see him jogging every morning. He's harmless. Going out running is all he thinks about.'

'Yeah, but what about the rumour that he wants to enter a marathon in Dupont? What if the Mayor told him it was never gonna happen? He'd be pretty pissed off I bet.'

'Yeah but Fleece, that doesn't mean he'd randomly poison half the colony.'

Up to this point Lieutenant Brett Dachshund has been taking in what's being said. Now he stands to offer his own opinion and lay down a strategy. All that confidence has started flooding his veins once more. He stands tall.

'OK. Now we're getting somewhere. Thanks to Bobby we can put Ferry Doberman at the crime scene just before mass. We also know that he was in a distressed state. However, being in a distressed state does not guarantee guilt. It could mean any number of things. Perhaps he had some bad news, or he had something on his mind unrelated to the poisonings. We don't know. Also, all of us were at the tea morning, practically the whole colony, and therefore all of us had the opportunity. Something could have been slipped into the tea at any point and by anyone.'

'Fuck.'

'What?'

'What is it Sun?'

'Mayor Harrier. It was really strange, he was going round helping Mrs Beagle serve the tea. He never does that. He did it for ages at the start, he was going round pouring for everyone. He never does that. (*starting to get upset*) And, fuck, Fleece do you remember? It was him, it was the Mayor who was stood right by Daisy when... and he was just stood there, not moving, not doing anything, and she was lying, shaking... it was him, he always hated her, it was him, I know it.'

'Calm down Sun, please, your language, think about it, think what your saying. I know, you're right, he was there; but that doesn't mean anything, it's not proof of anything. You're getting worked up. It's not good. We need to be rational and objective.'

'Yeah, I know, sorry Lieutenant.'

Now Deborah is excited.

'No, I like it Sun. This is gonna make a great story. Mayor poisons own people in New Luddle horror show. I can see it now. The Dupont Post, the Times, they're going to love it.'

'Shut up Deborah. You're gonna have to just... shut up.'

Deborah realizes how she must sound and it bothers her, for some reason it really bothers her. 'Oh, sorry.' She looks straight at him. 'Fleece, I'm sorry.'

The Lieutenant can see things are getting a bit heated. He calls for calm. He tells them they don't know anything for sure but accepts there are no closed possibilities.

'At some point this morning I will have to tell the Mayor that the NLPD is officially in action and on duty. I will gauge his reaction, if he has any guilt, it will show. Next, we need to speak to Ferry. He clearly knows something, no matter how small, we need to get it out of him. We'll grab him now, before he finishes his jog which is usually just before ten - as a matter of fact, he passes the police hut on his way home, so he'll be here in a few minutes. We'll grab him then. OK? Everybody calm? We need this to work, so lets take it easy and see how it plays out. You all just relax. Bobby? How about some tea.'

Once again Brett Dachshund has control of the situation. Sun, Fleece and Deborah sit and chat, knowing they mustn't jump to any conclusions until the facts are in. Having said that, Sun still suspects the Mayor has something to hide and Deborah thinks this Ferry Doberman sounds like a psycho; I mean spending all your time running around in the heat and the dust? It's enough to develop a murderous instinct in anyone. Fleece on the other hand is patient. He'll wait and see what happens. He would like justice. Justice for Daisy and justice for Geraldine Collie who was his friend and will now never get a chance to write the chronicles of New Luddle. He misses her and hopes Winston is OK. He'll go visit soon. He thinks how he'll immediately carry on with jibes and digs about recording New Luddle history, he won't mention Geraldine. He'll show that everything is normal without her. Everything is OK.

Sergeant Bobby Hound is making tea. He's in awe of his boss who hurriedly takes notes on what information and suspicions they have so far. There are circles and arrows all over the page. He knew the Boss was good but never thought he'd be quite this good. He's definitely going to pay more attention now. Now he's being taught by the best. That's what he'll tell his apprentice one day. 'I learnt from the best, kid. I learnt from a master.'

Ten minutes has passed and now they are all crowded round the police hut's little window at the front. Ten little eyes peering out of a small circle of space. And right on time, they see a ball of dust appear in the distance and a man running in front of it, leaving it all behind. An assured stride, there is no doubt about the athlete's identity. Lieutenant Brett Dachshund steps out onto the track and stops Ferry. He flashes the badge and escorts him into the hut. Deborah has moved the table and chairs to turn it into more of an interview room. She wants some ultra-bright light shining in Ferry's face but Fleece tells her not be so silly. It's New Luddle, not a torture chamber.

Ferry looks quite a picture in his shorts, his body laden in sweat. He is tall and skinny and usually full of twitches and nervy gesture. But Ferry strolls in to the hut without a care in the world. He is casual to the point of nonchalant.

'Hi Ferry.'

'Oh hi Sun. Hi Fleece, Bobby, er... sorry I'm not sure...'

'I'm Deborah. Deborah Jackal.'

'Oh. Hi Deborah.'

'Hello Ferry. You seem very chipper for someone who's just been brought in for questioning in a murder investigation.'

'Sorry?'

Bobby wants a taste of the action too.

'That's right Ferry. Now let's cut the crap and I'll see what I can do about cutting you a deal. (*pause*) erm, Boss is it OK to cut Ferry a deal?'

Brett Dachshund strides over with a cup of tea for Ferry, who doesn't seem to have taken much in thus far, in fact he hasn't stopped grinning since he entered the hut.

'What are you thinking Ferry? Do you not find it peculiar that a complete stranger is sat opposite you? Strangers aren't allowed in this colony Ferry, you know that yet you didn't blink an eye on being introduced. Then this complete stranger tells you you're being questioned in a murder investigation and you smile back, looking like you're in a dream world. What's going on Ferry?'

'You haven't heard? I'm going to be running in the Dupont marathon next month. Mayor Cudrip Harrier has agreed. It's true. I'll be there. I plan to win and bring glory to New Luddle.'

Deborah stands, pushing back her chair.

'What? And he says you can come back? Mayor Harrier said you could go run in a stupid race and then come back, no punishment, no catch?'

'Well, yeah. He says I can spend as long as I want there, treat it as a holiday he said. Then when I come back I can do a bit of work in the fields, but only part-time so I can practise my running. Can you believe it? I'm gonna be running in the Dupont marathon? It's really true.'

'But Ferry, are you sure? The Mayor wouldn't agree to this. Why would he agree to this.'

'Well. No. No I can't really talk about it actually. (*sudden change, no dream world anymore*) No please, I'm so happy, don't spoil it, it's all I've ever wanted to do really, run with others, with the Dupontians. Please, I can't really talk about it.'

And Ferry is scratching and rubbing his neck and getting all agitated.

'This is how he was that Saturday morning Boss. Just like it. All in a state. Rubbing, scratching – is he OK?'

'What do you know about the poisonings, Ferry?'

'Eh? What poisonings? What are you talking about?'

'Ken and Marjorie Setter, Daisy Spaniel, Gus Brindle and Geraldine Collie were all poisoned at the tea morning. We know that Ferry. And that's a crime, which is why myself and Sergeant Hound are investigating. The NLPD is real now, Ferry. We are genuine police officers with a lot of power and you have to tell us the truth. Now Bobby here saw you leaving the outhouse just before entering the church and you looked upset. What's going on Ferry?'

'Poisonings? You can't be serious. But the Mayor, he said it was one of those things – you get good luck and bad luck, the natural life cycle... no this can't be right, I mean yeah I was upset, I had to see Father Lurcher and he wasn't there, it was just Mrs Beagle. But poison? It wasn't to do with any poison. Listen, Lieutenant Dachshund, this cannot be right, I'm telling you: people do not get poisoned in new Luddle. Why are you questioning me? What have I done? I didn't mean to... what have I done wrong?'

Ferry is rubbing his neck so hard it's breaking the skin and he's starting to get really upset, starting to cry a little. Lieutenant Dachshund goes over and puts an arm round him.

'It's OK Ferry. We didn't mean to spoil your news. And it's great news, really great.'

Deborah screeches her chair on the wooden floor as she moves to look away, biting her bottom lip with fury. *I was dying and he wouldn't let us come back. Now he's letting them holiday. This place is meant to be fair, above all else it's meant to be fair.*

'But Ferry, this is serious: now we know you had nothing to do with the poisonings, of course you didn't. But we need to know what exactly it is you do know. It may help.'

'I hear what you're saying Lieutenant but I can't. I can't tell you anything and I can't tell you why. But it's got nothing to do with poisonings, I promise.'

Sun leans forward and urges Ferry to look at him.

'It's something to do with Mayor Harrier, isn't it Ferry? What do you know? Why is he letting you enter the marathon in Dupont? You've got to tell us Ferry.'

'I know. I know I should but I can't. I have to run in this marathon. I'm sorry I just have to. It was the only way... I just have to.'

Ferry stands and rushes to the door, he's full of tears and snot and sweat and he's mumbling about being sorry and how he didn't mean it because it was the only way and... he's gone. Nobody tries to stop him. He's gone.

Lieutenant Dachshund takes a deep breath.

'What's going on here? Can anyone tell me what's going on? Because this runs deep and Mayor Harrier is somewhere near the bottom of it.'

'I'd go as far to say he probably is at the bottom of it all, Boss.'

'Yeah, thanks Bobby.'

Sun lifts his head from the table, rubs his eyes and with two hands, scrapes back his hair.

'You think you know a place. You think you have security. You think any problems are theoretical, philosophical but none of it is true. Even a tiny little colony like ours – it's perfect then all of a sudden you find people are forced to leave, told they can never return just because they need help, and before you know it there's poisonings, liquor, dodgy deals... I'm pissed off. I am. Because a couple of months ago I was the happy, really happy. I was all happy and naive just like everyone else. Now I look at this place and see a wreck. And it's rotten, rotten to the core. How can that be?'

Fleece feels sorry for his friend. He would sometimes tell Daisy that Sun was naive, that he couldn't see past all the teachings and sunshine. She would have none of it. He's just a good person that's all Fleece, she'd say. He is sunshine.

Sun's little speech has put the unit into an apparent state of mourning. They were close to something for a second but now they don't have any idea what it was they were close to.

The Lieutenant jerks his neck to a funny angle and looks at Sun.

'Liquor? What liquor?'

'Oh yeah, I forgot to tell you about Ned Corgi and the liquor.'

They're back.

suspects gather for mass and tea, while the
unit watch on with expectations high

With Deborah impounded at the hut, the rest of the Unit stand at
the back of the St Bernard church for Pentecostal Pantheists for
the service. Each one of them has attended church every Saturday
for as long as they can remember and their thoughts while in
church on a Saturday have always been pretty much the same. Sun
- relaxed, happy. Fleece - bewildered, denial. Bobby - distant,
bored. Brett - focused, prepared. But now, today, on this Saturday
morning? Everything has changed. Everything is different. And
each member of the Unit knows that soon this whole thing is going
to explode in the face of every resident sat in this church. Very
soon this colony will undergo fundamental change, change that
will last forever. And it excites them.

Father Lurcher has finished his sermon and is now conjuring up
the Spirit so that he can inspire awe and speak in the language of
tongues. Everybody is ready to be astounded and amazed. But all
the Unit can see is the man who Ferry Doberman was desperate to
speak to on that day, and now Ferry can't say anything because it
would jepoardise his entering the marathon in Dupont, which
Mayor Harrier has unexpectedly allowed him to enter, which must
mean that Ferry has something on the Mayor and is only being
allowed to run the marathon on the condition he keeps his mouth
shut. But there is a good chance he sought counsel from Father
Lurcher before going to the Mayor and so Father Lurcher may well
know whatever it is Ferry knows, and the Mayor might not have got
to Father Lurcher yet, so if they can get to Father Lurcher first

before the Mayor they may be able to get all the information they need to wrap this whole thing up. That's what they see. One morning in the company of Lieutenant Brett Dachshund and that's all there is to see.

That, and the blackened banana that falls from the fruit cross and lands on Father Lurcher's head before sliding down onto his shoulder and sticking for two minutes, a record breaker. It's the banana Gerald Pinscher picked out before the sermon. He smiles and clenches a fist under the pew but cannot understand why his friend Gus Brindle isn't here with him. Why did he have to die with the others? Why one of my friends, my best friend? Why not Father Lurcher – he's such an idiot, why couldn't he have died?

He doesn't like playing the game on his own. He decides to split the points, giving half to Gus.

Soon the mass will be over and Sun, Fleece, Bobby and Brett will go to the tea morning, Brett will approach the Mayor to tell him they're in business, then they'll try and get some sense out of Father Lurcher before tackling the Ned Corgi situation.

It's all been arranged, they know what they have to do. But at this moment, Sun has a concern. Nothing links in with the poisoning. They seem to be investigating something else entirely. And looking out at the congregation, the usual faces all have a slightly more sinister look now. Sun glances over to Geoff Husky, a progressive school teacher, someone he admires, but all the playing around with that pipe, his yellow fingers – who's to be sure what really goes on in his mind all the time? It's the same with everyone, Kelly Chihuahua (well maybe not Kelly, it's highly unlikely she'll ever be able to give off an aroma of anything other than sweetness and innocence, yet with a knowing cheekiness that must exempt her from any possible ill doings). But all the others, the rest of the congregation. They're all capable of individual thought and motivation and who knows what that might be...? Sun shakes his head. Disappointment. So I'm a cynic now. Is this what

I really think? Suddenly all people are bad. No. I won't believe that. All people are good... but that doesn't mean bad things can't still happen.

****

Long, stretching rays of heat pounce as the church doors open and the residents make their way to the outhouse for tea. Father Lurcher continues the applause, his eyes shut, oblivious that everyone else has stopped and is leaving. The Unit lead the way but stay well apart from each other, Sun and Fleece take one side, Bobby and the Lieutenant the other. It is a fiercely bright morning and the residents all cover their eyes as they make the short journey to the out house where Mrs Beagle will have prepared everything as usual. It's the first tea morning Sun has been to since the poisonings. As he climbs the few steps and enters the wooden swing door, he feels a little dizzy, he begins to sway and swoon, but he knows there are things to be done and his passion is growing; there has been a definite switch in his mindset, a new determination to him, a conviction. He's taken on some of her traits; in some ways you could almost say he's becoming just like her because before long he's whispering and swearing in Fleece's ear. It's their task to accost Father Lurcher. It won't be easy.

The room is almost full. Mrs Beagle props open the swing door with a kettle full of cold water. Great shafts of light pile in as if trying to set fire to the floor but nobody seems to notice that. They each have a cup of tea and are gently chatting away. There is no sign of Father Lurcher yet. To the other side of the out house Lieutenant Brett Dachshund and Bobby Hound are having an equally difficult task trying to pin down Mayor Harrier. He seems to be working parts of the room that are impossible to penetrate without it looking clumsy and suspicious. But sooner or later they will speak with Mayor Harrier - Lieutenant Dachshund just hopes the same can be said for Sun and Fleece.

'I'm gonna have a quick word with Mrs Beagle, make sure he is coming.'

'OK, I need to speak with Winston Collie. I'll be quick, promise.'

Sun moves over to Mrs Beagle, who is stood by a table waiting for the tea to brew nicely.

'Hi Mrs Beagle.'

'Hello Sun, how are you doing today?'

'Oh, I'm OK thanks. Is Father Lurcher not coming over this morning?'

'Yeah, of course. He's the star isn't he? I'm sure he'll show.'

'Can I ask you a question Mrs Beagle?'

'Sure you can.'

'Do you think Father Lurcher can really speak in tongues? Because to be honest, there aren't many of us younger Ludlows who really believe in any of that. We think, well... we think he's just being a bit of a prat.'

Mrs Beagle laughs. Really laughs.

'Of course I couldn't possibly criticise Father Lurcher in any way so let's just say I didn't realize I had so much in common with the younger members of this colony.'

Sun is surprised he just said that. Mrs Beagle is delighted. It has made her day.

Only a few feet away Fleece Dingo is with Winston Collie, widower to Geraldine Collie.

'This is really important Winston, you have to listen to me and trust in what I am saying.'

'Not more local history Fleece, please, can we reminisce another day.'

'This isn't local history Winston, at least not yet.'

And finally, in the corner closest to the door, Mayor Cudrip Harrier is stood next to Lieutenant Brett Dachshund and Bobby Hound.

'What can I do for you gentlemen?'

'Well Sir, you remember the Jackal family?'

'Jackal family? No, not sure I do Brett.'

'Well, it was a long time ago. About fifteen years ago actually. They had a daughter, Deborah, only when she was a baby she got sick, real sick, and no one knew what was wrong with her. So the father, Tilson Jackal decided the only way to save Deborah's life was to take her over the border to Dupont, ringing any bells Sir?'

'Yes, of course (*crossness approaching anger*) look what is this Brett why are we talking about the Jackals? It was years ago.'

'Yes, fifteen Sir. Do you remember what you said would happen if any member of that family came back?'

'What? Yes, I said it would be a criminal offence and they would be arrested just as if they were a Dupontian, in fact that's what the Jackals are now, Dupontians, so why are we still talking about them?'

Go for it Bobby.

'Oh, it's because we have Deborah Jackal in custody back at the hut sir. She came back so we arrested her. Did a good job didn't we Boss?'

'We sure did Bobby.'

'But you can't arrest anybody, you're not real policemen, I mean...'

'Oh we are now Sir, we are real policeman now, but don't worry, everything's under control, we got it handled Mayor, isn't that right Bobby?'

'Oh yeah Boss, the colony's in safe hands now. I just hope that's the first and last crime to take place in the colony.'

The Mayor takes on a glazed look, in fact he looks quite peculiar. He can't quite believe what he's hearing.

'Well Bobby, we'll always be around now, just in case, now that it's all official, the NLPD will be everywhere. Don't worry Mayor, there'll be no stone unturned.'

'But... Deborah Jackal is here? In the police hut? right... OK, very well. Thanks. Yes thanks. We'll talk later.'

The Mayor stumbles into the crowd. Brett Dachshund turns to Bobby.

'Look at those footprints Bobby. What do they spell?'

'Spell? I don't understand, Boss.'

'They spell "guilt" Bobby. In big bright letters. They spell guilt.'

And while Bobby stares at the floor wondering what it is his mentor is talking about, Father Lurcher stands at the doorway, breathes in, breathes out, chest out, chin up, ready. He enters the room. It doesn't quite have the impact he was expecting, in fact it doesn't appear to have registered with anyone. They all continue to stand in little groups, holding their cups, nodding and laughing, smiling and doting. Except for two. Two teenagers have come rushing over with a pot of tea and a spare cup. They seem very excited by his arrival. At last, thinks Father Lurcher, perhaps the twenty minutes stood waiting outside in the heat wasn't wasted.

'Hi Father Lurcher, let me pour you some tea.'

'Thank you, yes don't mind if I do.'

Sun and Fleece are nervous, it goes awkward and quiet for a second. Father Lurcher looks expectant. Then it clicks. Fleece realizes first.

'Oh it was amazing Father Lurcher, really amazing, I just don't know how you do it, I mean every week, without fail – truly spectacular Father, really... amazing.'

'Thank you, you're too kind, well... anyway, it's a gift you see, when you're chosen like I have been it's a great responsibility, and the pressure! People don't understand the pressure. I'm more than God's voice, in many ways we're two separate people who happen to be doing the same job, it's like we're competing in a strange sort of way and it's tough because how do you say one persons better than another, I mean how do you quantify it? The only thing is, you don't really hear much about God 'the musician' and I feel if I've got an edge over him it's the music, I'll tell you actually only last night....'

Minutes pass, Sun and Fleece now appreciate the difficulty of their task. They need to take control of the situation. They need to get a word in.

'... and you think to yourself, is it a case of the pupil taking over from the master...?'

Sun has had enough.

'Father Lurcher, we know Ferry Doberman came to see you recently. He had something on his mind. What did he say to you?'

'Ferry Doberman? Did he? Oh yes, very upset he was. Of course he came to me for advice. Well, it wasn't a bad choice was it? Coming to me, ha ha!'

Sun and Fleece each do a fake laugh. Was it even a joke?

'Yes, now what was it? Oh, he'd seen something, early one morning, on one of his runs, down by the border, YES, that's it.'

Here we go. Sun and Fleece stand tight. Come on Father Lurcher let's have it.

'I remember perfectly now. I said Stop. Ferry, before you carry on, let me tell you what I see every night when I'm lying on my bed, because once I've told you what I've seen, I doubt you'll have the desire to compete. And so I told him boys, I told him my dreams and do you know what? I was right. He knew he wasn't going to match it and so he left. Actually, I think it had quite an impact on him, he left shaking and even, yes, there were definitely tears. It's my unique approach to narrative you see...'

Sun and Fleece just turn and walk. Their heads down, they don't even see Kelly Chihuahua wave hello to them. They find Brett and Bobby in the corner. The NLPD didn't require any of their specialist training to see that things hadn't gone well.

'Father Lurcher doesn't know shit. I think even Ferry caught on to the fact Father Lurcher isn't a good listener, he freaked out and left. But we were right about the Mayor. Ferry saw something one morning, by the border. It must have implications for the Mayor.'

'Yeah, I think you're right. We spoke to the Mayor. it was if one of us had punched him in the face. He didn't even really ask about Deborah, you could just tell from his face... it was like, I don't know, like he'd been caught already. But we still don't have anything. We need Ned Corgi.'

Sun and Fleece know that Ned is in a real mess right now. They know that if one of them went over to his house, they wouldn't get anything from him. And if Bobby and Brett went over, newly established and powerful or not, they could bring him in and do what they liked and still get nothing, because Ned Corgi doesn't care anymore. He doesn't care about anything. Well, of course we all know that isn't quite true.

Beth Pointer is sat on a stool near the door. She looks out onto an almost empty colony. She knows that while everyone else is in the outhouse, drinking tea, he is at home doing whatever, cooking, preparing, whatever it is he does on these Saturday mornings. Sun Saluki taps her on the shoulder. She turns and is glad it's a friend.

beth pointer goes to see ned corgi

Beth leaves the outhouse. Leaves them all drinking tea, being happy. She walks to Ned's. Along the dusty surface, dry and stony, smells of ripening tomatoes waft around in the sun which continues to beat down on New Luddle – but there's no aggression in the heat. Like everyone else, it's happy.

Sun has explained everything to Beth. How the plan worked, how everything was going to change. And he told her that Ned was at the heart of it. He needs rescuing Beth, you've gotta rescue him, please. That was how he put it. He said Ned was messed up. That he was losing it. She doesn't want him to lose it.

It's been many years since they spoke properly to each other. Several years since she looked him in the eyes, since she saw him proper. Like she used to see him.

The whole thing with Beth and Ned has been very unLudlow. You're meant to move on, just like that, forget the bad, remember everything is good. And that's generally how it is, but Ned and Beth. They can't forget. How can they move on when it's something that'll always be there?

She doesn't even knock on the door. She knows he's in the kitchen. There are clanging noises, pots and pans. She waits before going in. She's doing this because she has to. She's doing it to save him. She wants to see him again. That's why. She'd have taken any reason. There can't be any illusions here. It's all because she wants to see him again. She has to or she'll become the one losing it.

When he opens the door he sees her sat at a table, crying. Hands cover her face, shoulders jerk up and down. She's really crying.

'Beth? Is that you?'

She stands without removing her hands, her face still covered, she turns to leave, banging the table, kicking a chair.

'Beth? Beth! Please.'

He stands, serious, perfectly still, emotionless but for the thin lines of tears slipping from his cheeks.

They hold one another. For minutes and minutes they hold one another. She cradles his hand, touches the wooden limb with her lips, tasting every tomato dish he's ever cooked.

'What happened, Ned?'

'I don't know.'

'I'm sorry.'

'Yeah, me too.'

They sit, hands entwined on top of the table, staring, fascinated by the lines and creases, colours and movements of each other's faces.

'Your beard looks silly.'

'I'm older.'

'Silly older.'

'What does that mean?'

She shrugs. They're smiling now.

Ned makes tea. Beth looks out the window. She can see Mayor Harrier leaving the out house. He looks confused and anxious. She is glad he's going to be found out for whatever it is he's been up to. She knew all those things Daisy said were true. She always told Daisy to keep quiet. She'll speak up for her now, be her voice. She knows she has to find out what this mess Ned has gotten himself involved in is. Sun was right. He will tell her. He'll tell her everything and then, maybe, everything can start again.

*when mayor cudrip harrier went to ned
corgi's to be persuaded to let him open
ned's night and quit working in the fields*

Everything was set. Eight dishes. They were all there. Crimson classic, Vintage Vermillion and a very special tomato soup Ned had been working on for weeks. The Mayor arrived bang on time.

'You're wasting your time with this Ned.'

'Just try it Mayor, you might be surprised.'

'What's this one?'

'That's a Ravishing Ruby, Mayor.'

The Mayor sat at a table on his own and gradually worked his way through each dish.

It was strange because he'd been telling anyone who'd listen how this Ned's Night was never going to happen. 'It's not the New Luddle way,' he would say. 'A dashed cheek that Ned Corgi's got.' But regardless of this he would always be told just how delicious the food Ned created was. And despite saying how this was beside the point, he was really tucking in now. A napkin scrunched in behind his tie, he leant over his bowl and simply gobbled the lot. All eight dishes.

'What do you call this one Ned?'

He was pointing to the soup. A brand new dish, the Mayor had been the first to try.

'I don't know yet, it's new.'

The Mayor stood with a very serious face, contemplating.

'Well, I think it's the one Ned.'

'The one?'

'The one we're going to market and sell to the Dupontians.'

'Sorry, what?'

'That's if you want this Ned's Night thing to happen, of course.'

'But we can't do that. We can't trade with them!'

'That's a fine soup you've got there Ned. There's 250 million Dupontians who'd get a real kick out of it – big money too.'

'But it's against the rules, it's illegal. You can't do it Mayor Harrier, even if you wanted.'

'Ned, listen up...'

The Mayor reaches into his top pocket. He pulls out a quarter bottle of liquor and a packet of cigarettes.

'Where'd you get those?'

'Where'd you think, Ned?'

He pours two large measures and lights a cigarette. He throws the pack back onto the table and pushes a glass to Ned.

'Now you take a drink Ned, you take a drink and listen to me. I'm the Mayor of this fucking backward shanty town, I'm in charge. Nobody has to know about any of this. You make the soup, you put it in boxes, you store it in your new restaurant. Once a month we take the boxes to the border and get them picked up. In exchange we get some of this (points to bottle) and bit of that (cigarettes) plus, I get some money and you get to live your dream with this place. I know all about you and Beth, I know that's over and it's got to be hard for you. This stuff helps (bottle), believe me, it helps. I'll leave this bottle with you, there's plenty more available. Now if you're not comfortable with this Ned, if you think it's wrong or immoral or whatever, you just say. That's fine. But do you really want to go back to those fields? You really want to turn down the opportunity for Ned's Night? It's up to you. Think about it. I'm going to fill my bowl with some more of this delicious soup.'

The fact was, Ned had become so determined to make Ned's Night work he'd have done anything for it. After the initial shock, the idea of selling soup to the Dupontians didn't seem so bad. And he'd gotten sick of the whole New Luddle life since the break-up with Beth and leaving the fields. He just wanted to spend his days cooking, he didn't care about anything else. So what if it's illegal? Nobody will find out, he thought. I've got the Mayor backing me. He can do what he wants. It'll be fine.

And this liquor is good. It's like he said. It helps.

'So what's it to be Ned? Are you in?'

'I'm in Mayor Harrier.'

'Excellent news. Oh, but Ned, I perhaps should have said. If you tell anyone about this then I'll doubtless end up killing you. I'm quite serious about that.'

After letting this fact set in the Mayor quickly lets a smile open up round his face, he pours more drink.

'To a lasting partnership.'

Ned downs it in one and reaches for the bottle.

'A lasting partnership.'

*the unit head to ned's to see if they can
finally find out what the hell has been
going on in new luddle seeing as everyone
else who might know is useless*

Tea morning is over. The Unit rush over to Ned's, anxious to see if
Beth has managed to get anything out of him. When they arrive
Ned is whistling and wiping down all the tables.

'Hey, how are you all?'

Wariness blankets all four of The Unit.

'Congratulations by the way Lieutenant Dachshund, Sergaent
Hound. I'm glad you're going to finish this. Can I get anyone
something to eat?'

'No thanks Ned, erm, where's Beth? She has been here, right?'

'Oh yeah, she's in the kitchen pouring liquor down the sink.
Listen, I'm OK. Me and Beth have had a long chat. Everything will
be fine. Please sit. I'll tell you everything.'

Beth comes out from the kitchen drying her hands with a cloth.
She is smiling.

'Hey, how is everyone?'

She looks positively ecstatic. It is very confusing.

'Fine thanks Beth, Ned here was just going to explain what's
been going on.'

'Oh great. All out in the open. Everything is going to be fine
Ned, just fine. Tell them.'

Ned explains everything. How the Mayor came for a tasting session
and convinced him to produce the soup for market. How he

brought over liquor and convinced him to drink. Ned took responsibility for his actions though. He told them how he didn't really take much convincing. He was desperate for Ned's Night to become a reality and this was the only way. So once a month he would box up amounts of soup and pass them over the border.

All of a sudden it all became clear to Sun: the boxes in the kitchen, Ned's face that night. Sat on the steps, spitting, swearing, apologising. His face was so tired, racked with guilt and hurt. So unrecognisable to the man sat here, now, telling the tale like it's from a story book, always glancing over to Beth, she always glancing back. Ned carries on. He talks about the border exchanges. How two men with a truck would always come to meet him and the Mayor at the border. Ned would never speak, just load the truck with the boxes. It would be very early in the mornings; sometimes it was scarcely light. The Mayor would stand and have a cigarette with the Dupontian men. He was always telling the men stories about New Luddle – he'd try and mythologise it to the men, exaggerate stories, make New Luddle out to be an extreme puritanical community where people can only speak when it's daylight and aren't allowed to eat during the winter. Ridiculous stuff. He had a plan, you see. He was always telling the men that in five years New Luddle would be officially open to the Dupontian public. Visitors would be able to live like a Ludlow as part of one-week package excursions. The Mayor intended to rent out empty accommodation for a very high price but in return Dupontians would get the full authentic experience: attending church, growing tomatoes and drinking tea. A completely alternative way of life. It was his grand plan. Ned never paid that much attention to him. Except for the exchange they made the day after the tea morning. The Mayor was so excited he couldn't wait to tell the men about how they had a mass murderer in the colony, spate of poisonings at the tea morning: five dead, it was the biggest thing ever to happen in New Luddle history, he told them.

'I couldn't believe he was talking about Daisy and everyone else, like their deaths were great news because it was another story he could tell the men. It's like he couldn't have planned anything better to get the Dupontians really interested. They love a good murder, he'd say, now how about five at once? I confronted him afterwards but he laughed. Said he could easily take away the liquor and put me back in the fields just like that. He was right, too. He's got all this money they use in Dupont. I think once he's set up New Luddle as a business he wants to move to Dupont. I heard him asking one of the men if he owned a swimming pool and saying he'd like to spend a whole day with a pina colada in his hand. He's going to farm us to the Dupontians and live their life with the profits. I'm pretty sure that's the plan.'

The Unit are shocked to see Beth and Ned speak so casually about this. They don't seem to have a care in the world. The Unit on the other hand need to take in all this information and act. Of course it's the Lieutenant who manages to get to this stage first.

'You realize that I should arrest you, Ned. You've been complicit in all of this – exporting soup, smuggling and consuming liquor. I believe the Mayor did put extreme pressure on you but that doesn't change the facts of the matter. You've been committing crime for months on end, Ned.'

Beth looks to Lieutenant Brett Dachshund and speaks slowly.

'That wasn't Ned, not really. He was a mess. I was a mess. I'd have done the same. It's different now. He didn't even flinch when I poured the liquor away but last night it was all he cared about. It's over Lieutenant. Please, just let us be happy again. Please.'

Being the pro he is, and seeing how everyone has experienced this first-hand in the last few hours, it came as a great surprise when Lieutenant Brett Dachshund burst out laughing. Bobby in particular couldn't believe it. He'd been touched by Beth and Ned's devotion to one another, he hoped one day he'd find that.

Now it looked like it could all come to an end if the Boss locked Ned up in prison.

'This is New Luddle. I'm not going to lock good people up. I don't intend to lock anyone up. Prison isn't for people who've made mistakes. It's for those in the process of making mistakes, it's there to stop them making any more. Ned you've given us everything we need. We've got the Mayor on any number of counts, we've got him.'

Sun stands.

'He'll be charged with murder though right? We know he did it, like Ned was saying, he wanted to put New Luddle on the map, create an interest for the Dupontians. He has to be guilty, I mean we're going for it aren't we?'

'I'm not sure we can prove it Sun, unless he confesses I don't see how we'll ever know for sure. You're right though, we have motive now. We finally have motive.'

Fleece claps his hands together. The unravelling of the mystery has been enthralling. Fleece feels the andrenalin.

'So what now?'

Before Lieutenant Dachshund can answer his sergeant steps forward.

'We go get the Mayor.'

There is a uniform nod of agreement between The Unit, they raise their chests, finish their tea and prepare for action. Beth and Ned are oblivious to any of this. They don't even notice as The Unit move over to the door.

'So where will he be, at home?'

'Possibly, but he knows he's in trouble and he's going to want to find out how much trouble. He hasn't been here, my guess is he probably went to see Ferry first, see if he's talked. Assuming he believes Ferry when he tells him he hasn't, he'll come here and warn Ned not to say anything. We could just wait.'

'OK, sounds good. We wait.'

They move back to the table and take a seat. Beth stands.

'I'll make some more tea if you're staying for a bit.'

'Thanks Beth.'

'Of course, I saw the Mayor earlier.'

'Yeah, where?'

'Leaving the tea morning. You must have really frightened him Lieutenant because he looked in a right state.'

'Where was he going Beth?'

'Well it was while the tea morning was going on. I don't know, it looked like he was going towards your police hut.'

Almost instinctively Fleece stands up and shouts.

'Deborah!'

He's out the door before Sun, Bobby and the Lieutenant can say anything to stop him. They chase after him knowing that the Mayor could be extremely dangerous.

The sun pours out its rays as they sprint in the dust. Fleece will not be caught; big clouds of dust hide his position in front, particles slip into the eyes and hair of the pursuing group. Sun is worried that his friend will be in danger, Lieutenant Dachshund doesn't want any ugly scenes, and Bobby... Bobby is loving this, he's absolutely loving it.

With the hut in sight, Fleece is screaming Deborah's name, he's picturing how this is all going to play out: he'll barge the door down, duck below the Mayor's first punch, land one in his stomach to wind him then, as he's gasping for air, kick down hard on the knees to send him scuttling along the floor. Then he'll grab the terrified but relieved Deborah in his arms and say something like: 'It's ok, it's ok, he can't hurt you now.' Perfect.

Fleece reaches the door. Without even slowing his stride he crashes through and the momentum sends him down onto the floor. Desperately scrambling to get some footing he is eventually brought to a stop – by a chair leg which impacts his head and leaves him lying still on his back, waiting for vision to return. When it does he sees that not two feet away and in a similar position on the floor is Mayor Cudrip Harrier.

Sun, Bobby and the Lieutenant reach the hut. Deborah is sat by the window drinking tea.

'Alright team, how we doing.'

'Deborah what happened to the Mayor? Is he... dead?'

'Dead? I doubt it. Clattered him over the head with this that's all. He'll be alright.'

'Deborah that's a steel card container. Goodness me. Look – it's all bent. The cards are all bent too. You can't play gin rummy with these.'

'Oh, sorry.'

Lieutenant Dachshund laughs.

'You OK?'

'Yeah, he's a coward really – came in threatening me with all sorts. I thought it was funny. I kept telling him what a great end to the piece this was going to make. He got so cross he took off that stupid bowler hat and tried to throttle me. I just picked up what was nearest.'

'He could have killed you Deborah.'

'Hardly.'

'Sure you're OK? Not in shock or anything?'

'I'm fine.'

A noise comes from the floor.

'Ahem.'

It's Fleece.

'Oh, hello down there.'

Sun is laughing.

'He came to rescue you Deborah.'

'So I saw. You were awesome Fleecy.'

'Yeah, yeah very funny.'

'My hero.'

'Look I wasn't trying to rescue you, I couldn't care less. No, it was more the capture of Mayor Harrier I was concerned about really... I knew you'd be fine.'

Fleece and Deborah laugh. Resigned to humiliation he takes a seat by her side. She looks at him and a little droplet of tear clings to her eye.

'I heard you call my name. I could hear every word.'

Fleece can't be sure but that seemed like a sign that maybe she's warming to him. That's good he thinks, shit that's really good. He gets up to make some tea. He resists the urge to rub his head – that would just draw attention to the fact he was such an idiot. Deborah called the Mayor a coward. That's what I've been for years. I should have listened to Daisy. I should have spoken out. I'm not going to be a coward again. I can't be.

Lieutenant Brett Dachshund bends down and secures handcuffs to Mayor Harrier's hands and feet.

'Will we lock him up forever Boss?'

'I say we set him free Bobby.'

Everyone turns to Lieutenant Dachshund, they are stunned.

'What?'

'In New Luddle we get on with things. We don't dwell and we don't punish ourselves or others for things that have happened. There is no prison in New Luddle, just this hut and I for one don't intend to build one. He will leave New Luddle and never be allowed back. Extradition is good enough for us.'

'But he killed, he killed Daisy and all the others.'

'Did he? Let's see. Let's see if he admits it when he wakes up. I bet he won't. It doesn't fit, Sun. He had a carefully worked out plan; it was about using New Luddle to make money and be rich in Dupont. I don't think he wanted to kill people. He doesn't care enough to want them dead. He's nasty and conniving but I'm not sure he's a killer.'

Fleece brings over five cups of tea on a tray.

'He definitely did it.'

'I agree. Deborah?'

'Of course he did, you know it too Bobby.'

'They've got a point Boss, I agree. He's guilty of those poisonings, it was all part of the plan. It has to have been.'

'Maybe. It's certainly possible, but I don't think so.'

Lieutenant Brett Dachshund's leadership, decision making and police skills have been so impressive all day that they have all built up a huge respect for him and like him a lot. He'd been right on just about everything during this whole investigation and because of this, Fleece, Sun, Deborah and Bobby couldn't be absolutely sure. In their own minds it was a certainty but how could they be sure if Brett Dachshund wasn't? It was annoying.

'Somebody had better go and check on Ferry.'

'Why – Ferry's alright isn't he?'

'I doubt it. Bobby, would you mind going?'

'Sure Boss, sure.'

There's an air of sadness to it all as Bobby leaves to go see Ferry. Everyone goes quiet. Sun picks up the bowler hat that Mayor Harrier threw down. He thinks about Victor Poodle and all that New Luddle history, the creation of a New Luddle way. It'll have to change. Everything will have to change.

some sadness and some hope

Ferry's house is the one nearest to the police hut. Bobby knocks on the door. He can hear people crying inside.

'Hello Sergeant.'

'What's happened Donny?'

Ferry is lying on his bed. He doesn't really have any expression. Bobby walks in. They exchange glances. Ferry lifts the bedsheet and Bobby sees the broken bone and hacked flesh that make up Ferry's legs.

'He said I shouldn't have talked. That he wasn't joking when he said I'd never run again.'

Bobby takes a deep breath. He feels the inside of his pocket, where his police badge is. It's for real now. He turns to Ferry and smiles.

'Nonsense. You're going to be fine Ferry Doberman. A few minor scrapes like that. Bit of training you'll be back in no time. We have the Mayor, there's no need to worry. You're safe. Everyone's safe now. This is New Luddle. Everything will be fine. Now let's make you a cup tea, and how about a little slice of tomato cake eh? It's some beautiful weather out there...'

While Bobby rises to the challenge and cheers up the Doberman household, Mayor Cudrip Harrier comes round. He doesn't say a word. Even when he's told he will escape punishment in New Luddle, that he will be banished to wherever he likes, he doesn't speak. Even Deborah Jackal asking for a quote to use in her article, a radiant smile blooming on her face, doesn't get a reaction. Everything is explained to him. He doesn't speak.

Sun wishes Daisy could be here. He wishes he knew what her and the Mayor were talking about just before she died. He recognises Mayor Harrier's silence. He is just how he was when Daisy lay on the floor. Still, motionless, not speaking. As far as Sun is concerned it's the guilt. It's grabbed hold of him. Sun hopes it won't ever let go, but he knows it probably will. To be honest he doesn't care. Like it or not, he's a Ludlow, a Ludlow through and through. Soon the Mayor will be gone and everything can change. Sun feels this was perhaps all that Daisy wanted, for him to be gone and a freedom for change. Now it's happened and he isn't sure, but from somewhere inside he can feel her slipping away, hair tied back, happy again. Sun smiles.

END OF PART TWO

friday morning with sun saluki

There is a bridge in New Luddle that stretches out over a busy commuter track. Cars and trucks grumble and shit along its uneven surface but the drivers - the Dupontians - don't ever look up.

They don't ever see the boy who stands on this bridge looking down.

The boy is called Sun Saluki and he likes to look for slogans. He hasn't seen any in a while. In truth, it isn't really the reason he goes up there every day, he just says that because he doesn't want to tell the truth.

Sun never met his father, Bryce Saluki. Before Sun was born Bryce jumped off the bridge and onto the busy commuter track. Every day Sun stands on the bridge and wonders why he would have done that knowing Sun was about to be born. Surely that would be reason enough to stay on the bridge. He's learnt a lot more about his dad recently. Sun knows what New Luddle could do to people of that generation. But he wishes Bryce had stayed around, maybe fought back a little. Certainly if he was around today he wouldn't be sad, he wouldn't feel that way now. If only his dad were born after him, he'd be fine then. He wouldn't have to hide in tomato fields to talk freely. If Bryce Saluki had been born after his son, he would have been fine.

Leaving treads in the dust, Sun Saluki walks away from the bridge towards home. He sees Tala Pekepoo going into Beth and Ned's cafe. 'Enjoy your breakfast Tala.' She waves back and smiles. A few beads of sweat start to swell on the back of Sun's neck. Today it's hot. Really hot. The sun is parading itself for all to see and yet it's still early. Everybody loves it though. Everyone is happy. Sun approaches his house. He can see Ferry Doberman stretching.

'Hey Ferry, how are the legs?'

'Getting there thanks Sun. I'm aiming for the Dupont marathon in three years.'

'We're with you all the way Ferry, with you all the way.'

Inside, Sun wipes some of the dust from his shoes and heads into the kitchen. The window is open and there are some flowers on the table. Sun can smell tea and tomatoes.

'Morning mum.'

Jennifer turns from the sink and smiles at her son.

'Happy birthday Sun. How do you feel?'

'Yeah, good thanks.'

'Something came for you today.'

'Really? what?'

'A letter.'

'But... how?'

'I'm not sure, it was just there on the mat by the door.'

Sun takes a seat and opens the letter. He's never received one before.

Fleece Dingo
23 Eastern Block
Avenue 8
Revenue Hill
Dupont

Dear Sun,

Happy birthday, sorry I can't be there today. It's been too long since we met up. I know you're fundamentally changing the beliefs and principles of New Luddle (must be tiring) but really that's no excuse not to pop round for a cup of whatever it is they call tea here. Me and Deborah have our own flat now. It has rats and damp and the water doesn't so much run as fall down now and again. It's great. Spoke with some publishers last Friday and they seem really keen about my New Luddle history book. It's funny, I was rereading through some passages and I remembered just how amazing a place New Luddle is. This is going to sound stupid, but please don't change it too much. Don't take away the happiness at least. Hardly anyone is happy here. Pretty much it's just me and Deborah. And the very rich. Oh and Tilson and Maggie. They are always asking after you and your mum. When you sort out this immigration visa thing you're doing I think Jennifer should come over and see them. Tilson talks about your dad all the time. I know you wished things were different but Tilson says you should be proud, it was your dad who sowed the seeds for everything. Tilson says he was the first free-thinking man in the history of New Luddle and the best friend anyone could want. He's getting a whole chapter in the book. I hope you don't mind.

I'll try and visit soon, illegally or not. I miss you and Daisy. I miss you lots.

Say hello to everyone in that perfect happy society of yours. Miss you all.

Fleece.

It's only when he's outside that Sun begins to cry. He hopes the heat will dry his face quickly without leaving marks. There is still lots to do. He'll meet up with Fleece and Deborah soon. First he needs to make his way to the fields and do a good day's work. He needs to prove himself to all the residents in this colony if he wants to get their votes.

The sun is hot. It stretches out. In the air is the smell of tomatoes and tea. Behind one of the doors is the sound of laughter. Everyone is happy. In New Luddle, everyone is happy.

THE END

Printed in the United Kingdom
by Lightning Source UK Ltd.
131596UK00001B/16-54/P